THE QUAGMIRE

A Micro-Fiction Anthology

THE QUAGMIRE

Mystery and Suspense Stories from Unexpected Places

JORGE A. ONTIVEROS

HISPANIC INSTITUTE OF SOCIAL ISSUES

MESA, ARIZONA • 2025

FIRST EDITION

The Quagmire
Mystery and Suspense Stories from Unexpected Places

Copyright © 2025 Jorge A. Ontiveros

Hispanic Institute of Social Issues
123 N. Centennial Way, Suite 105
Mesa, AZ 85201
(480) 939-9689 | HISI.org

Cover & book interior designed by Yolie Hernandez
yolie@hisi.org

Cover photo by Omar Jabri

Library of Congress Control Number: 2025930265

Paperback ISBN: 978-1-936885-61-9

To my daughter, Marisol Brown Ontiveros.
Thank you for your patience in proofreading
and for your invaluable feedback.

Contents

THE QUAGMIRE

The Best Pool Player in the World

IT WAS THE YEAR 1930, OR MAYBE 1932; THE EXACT YEAR ISN'T KNOWN. According to historical accounts, this renowned individual challenged the best pool players in the major capitals of South America and the Caribbean, from Havana to Port-au-Prince, betting substantial sums of money. He would start in Buenos Aires and then move on to Santiago de Chile. He began in the fall to avoid the harsh winter temperatures. His matches were advertised in the Valparaíso newspaper, La Gazeta, or in El Mercurio of Chile: "One night only—prove you're the best. Bets range from $1,000 to $5,000."

This man, known as Rudy, was a well-organized player. A seasoned accountant with a sharp intellect named Tom traveled with him, coordinating the dates with various casinos. Usually, each venue had seven to ten players betting between $1,000 and $5,000, including two burly men. People said they were Samoans, but one was actually Hawaiian. Each month, they received ten percent of the winnings plus expenses, while the accountant took fifteen percent.

After fifteen years of never losing a game, a dark-skinned man with a stern personality appeared. Rudy not only played about thirty games against him but ultimately lost for the first time. The newspapers made a big deal about his defeat, but then they fell silent because The Dapper Man—named for his distinctive attire—never showed up to claim his winnings, which were rightfully earned. Later, in Lima, reporters claimed it was all a publicity stunt. The truth was that Rudy felt insecure and spoke to Tom.

"Next year, find me this man. I want to get my revenge. I'm the mathematician of the table; my geometry is perfect. I know, down to the millimeter, where the cue ball will land and can make it backtrack at will. To this day, no one has embarrassed me after winning more than two hundred and fifty games."

The day for Rudy to play against the Dapper Man again came, but this time in a city south of Buenos Aires. The game was not publicized; they played for seven days and nights, indifferent to the passage of time. The prize was $5,000, a substantial sum at that time. Exhausted, the Dapper Man would sometimes take the lead, while at other times, Rudy would.

As the final night of the seventh day drew to a close, dawn was just beginning to break. The Dapper Man had the eight ball, the fateful black ball, ready to sink and end the game, defeating Rudy and stripping him of his fame and money. He struck with fury, his sole aim to hit the black ball, sink it, win, and collect. But fate's hand would not allow it; he barely touched the black ball. The Dapper Man took off his hat, dusted the chalk off his hands, and disappeared through the door.

"I won! I won!" Rudy shouted.

"You didn't win!" Tom said, bringing Rudy back to reality. "Even when he lost, he was still your mentor. He took you off the streets when you were just seven years old and taught you how to make a living easily. You didn't recognize him! He came to greet you and, in doing so, gave you one final lesson."

Somewhere in South America, snowflakes swirled around Rudy and his team as they made their way by train to Ecuador.

I Died Three Times

ICOME FROM A POOR FAMILY IN NORTHERN MEXICO. FACING SEVERE financial hardship, I began working as a miner when I was eighteen. In my town, there were only a few ways to make a living: as a priest, a thug, or a miner. I chose the latter because the first two went against my nature.

I don't believe in premonitions, but for months, I dreamed of riding in a taxi, crossing a bridge, and returning, upset because I didn't have the money to pay for the ride.

I was an outcast, never really getting along with anyone. I preferred to work at night, sometimes deep underground, breaking rocks to extract valuable minerals and bring them to the surface. Other times, I watched over overflowing water tanks to keep them from spilling. I had no choice but to endure the bitter cold that seeped into my bones, with only a small candle for warmth, which seemed to burn down to my soul.

Every night, I dreamed of the same person driving me in a taxi from one side of the river to the other. I could never see his face, only feel the cold of his hand when I handed him the coin before reaching the other side. But before I could reach the shore, the driver would take me back to where I started.

One night, deep underground, I was sent to shut off the water valve of a reservoir. I squeezed through a narrow wooden hole, barely able to move through. The space was tight—just about ten meters in every direction. Heavy railroad sleepers protected the area against falling rocks or potential collapses. I managed to reach and close the valve, but on my way back, I got stuck. I couldn't move forward, and I didn't want to panic. I tried to back up but couldn't make any progress. My cries were muffled by the confined space, and to make matters worse, it was Friday. All my co-workers would go home and forget about me. I would have to wait there until Monday, crammed like a mouse in a trap designed just for me. Hours passed.

I was running out of oxygen, sweat pouring from every pore. Everything grew darker, slowly and distressingly, as if the shadows advanced sluggishly under the weight of their own mist. The terrifying confinement overwhelmed me. I slowly inched backward, unsure whether it was morning or night, until I finally emerged. As I struggled to free myself, the darkness closed in, and just as I felt I could no longer breathe, I suddenly found myself in the sacristy of a church, a place I had never seen before in the mine. I had emerged right where they repaired religious figures. I saw a dozen or so pink angels with real, lifelike eyes. Some were statues of saints. They seemed to follow me with their gaze. I touched them; they felt like plaster or alabaster. I left them all there in that strange room and peeked into another. Inside, I found my grandmother, sitting on her bed, dressed in white with her thick, gray hair.

"Are you back from work, son?" she asked.

"Yes, Grandma."

"Bring me some water from the still."

I went to fetch her water with a cup that had no handle; it was so worn I almost tore the bottom out just trying to fill it.

"Go and have dinner before you go to sleep."

I ate a bit of meat with bread and coffee—the kind of meal I had on weekends.

"Grandma 'Ala,'" I said affectionately (her name was Manuela), "you died a long time ago. Why are you here?"

"I don't know. You should go to sleep and put everything in order."

"Grandma, I'm feeling so sentimental. Sing me a song."

"From the flowers of my garden, filled with sadness and pain…,'" my grandmother sang—"filled with sadness and pain, I keep a jasmine for you, and with it, I give you my love, and with it, I give you my heart…"

I lay down on that bed, which smelled of cleanliness and love. I wondered, "Where am I?" and drifted off between illusion and dream. I traveled to other lands, places where illusions are born. I arrived at the place from where I came, saw myself when I was nothing—no name, not even a dream—but I couldn't see myself. I sat on a park bench. There she was, close to me; I could feel her face, her enchanting smile. "Why don't you say anything?"

She smiled with a beautiful gaze, lost in the distance. I realized she was dead—her icy hands told me so, and her new, freshly bought clothes were for those who had passed on. I got up and left behind that love of my youth. The park's leaves were black, and a small gust of wind swept through. I felt a deep sadness for being alone. I couldn't find anyone; I was alone, immensely alone, lost on the path of life.

I reached the starting point; I arrived back in my town. I walked through the fog. I reached Alfareña Street, where the houses of my childhood stood, with cracked parapets, streets shrouded in fog, all enveloped in darkness. I arrived at my humble home; I felt like an intruder. I saw a wood-burning stove with a fire that was nearly out. My brothers, Javier and Víctor, were asleep, but I wasn't there. My mother woke up.

"Son, what are you doing here?"

"I don't know, Mom. I'm lost. Everything is gone. I went to the movies to distract myself but found nothing—no town, no cinema, just fog. Mom, I'm alone; I can't find anyone. What should I do?"

"My son, come here so I can give you my blessing. You're lost, but I'm your mother, in life and in the afterlife. Go find someone to guide you."

This was incomprehensible; I fell asleep on a journey to infinity. When I woke up, I was on a metallic table. Some people looked at me as if I were a stranger, perhaps because I was in a very cramped refrigerator. I felt like I was going to suffocate. I could hear people speaking to me from the sides.

"Hey, you! Are you there? Don't pretend; we know you're there!"

"Scumbag, here you're nothing, just human waste! Part of you is already in the blender."

"Who are you?"

I was filled with fear. The next day, I was still in that metallic box. From there, I heard voices.

"Answer!"

"This idiot came in all nervous to buy one of those cases, and when he tried it on, he got stuck. But the box didn't have a lock inside. What killed him was the fear, poor fool!"

I heard everything, but it was too late. I was already on the other side of the mountain, and I had paid the taxi driver to take me across the bridge.

Code Blue

WHEN I AWOKE FROM AN INDUCED COMA, I FOUND MYSELF TRAVELING from the Region of Lagoons, passing through Torreón, Gómez Palacio, and Lerdo, in the state of Coahuila, Mexico. The food markets were eerily empty—no fruit, no people, no rats, nothing! It felt as if everyone had fled either north or south, or as though some catastrophe had struck. I gathered whatever I could: cans, weapons, matches—anything to survive.

I headed north, a direction where I've always felt strong. I got lost in the arid zones; I think I was somewhere in Durango. I saw rivers of dust and dust storms, along with a great number of objects strewn across the landscape, left behind by people during their exodus: shoes, backpacks, empty cans. I had no idea where they were going. Among the abandoned things, there was a palpable sense of despair, anxiety, and fear.

Over time, I lost my fear and gained a greater appreciation for life. Eventually, I reached a desert area where even the most insignificant things were treasures, worth their weight in gold: matches, courage, water, and other essentials.

I saw few survivors; those I did encounter were stealing whatever they could get their hands on—good jackets, sturdy boots, anything useful. Because of my height and youth, no one tried to mess with me. It was then I learned the art of bartering, once exchanging matches and a can of plums for a piece of meat.

I ventured deeper into the desert—I don't know what state it was. Wrapped in a snowstorm, I found a cantina called "The Code Blue." "How funny," I thought. "I could write a song about this."

In the distance, I saw a hospital where the urgent calls of 'Code Blue! Code Blue!' echoed through the air. As I continued wandering deeper into the mystical desert, I couldn't stop repeating the phrase to myself, 'Code Blue! Code Blue!'

CODE BLUE: A hospital emergency code indicating that a patient is in critical condition and needs immediate medical attention.

The Swap

DAWN WAS BREAKING IN ARIZONA, AND THE SUN WAS RELENTLESS FOR travelers moving from one city to another. It was advised to carry water because if a car broke down on the road, one could perish under the scorching sun before help arrived.

A group of people had crossed the border illegally three days earlier. They were waiting for the "coyotes"—the human smugglers who had left them in a dangerous area. This group of fourteen men had entered the United States from Mexico. The coyotes, those shady characters who, for a hefty fee, guide you through the desert to safety, took their money and, under the pretense of going to get water, abandoned their human cargo. Two brothers in the group began to fight.

"We're out of water."

"You drank it all."

"No! It was you."

The older brother hit the younger one twice, knocking him down into the scorching sand.

"Get up and fight, you bastard."

The younger brother grabbed a handful of sand and threw it in his brother's face, temporarily blinding him. Taking advantage of the moment, he kicked him in the stomach, causing him to writhe in pain. Among the onlookers, a one-eyed man with a menacing look tossed a small dagger—a long-bladed knife that glinted in the sun.

"Kill that bastard, slit his throat."

Toribio, the younger brother, looked at the one-eyed man, grabbed the dagger, and threw it with all his might into one of the bushes.

"I should have killed you, you devil of a one-eyed man. Get up, brother, I'm sorry, I lost my temper," Toribio said as he helped Matthias to his feet.

"Don't worry, brother, you gave me a good kick, knocked the wind out of me," Matthias replied.

"You're my older brother, and I owe you respect," Toribio said.

"Let's go to the shade of that saguaro cactus and wait for the pair of thieves who stole our money."

They all fell asleep, hungry, thirsty, and lost. The desert sand, turning into a wind of death, loomed ominously.

* * *

Toribio awoke in a cool, serene temple. The first thing he saw was a fountain with crystal-clear water that appeared blue from a distance. He remembered his father, who, after a day's labor, would lie down and drink from a babbling stream.

"Son, move the leaves and tadpoles aside, put your whole face into the water and drink as much as you need."

In the temple, Toribio drank from the fountain until he was satisfied. In this temple with statues and gigantic columns, he estimated that a dozen men holding hands could barely encircle one of the Herculean columns. There were hundreds of Doric columns holding up a ceiling that one could not circumnavigate in days, nor find the way out if someone tried. He sat and waited to see what would happen. After a few hours, he got up and decided to walk, not wanting to lose sight of the water. When it seemed the fountain was disappearing in the distance, he would return. After several days, he sat down to rest when he saw someone approaching from afar—it was a janitor.

"Hey, I know you. You're the one-eyed man from Windmill Mountain Desert in Arizona," Toribio said.

"I don't know you. I just clean this temple, and to finish cleaning it completely, it will take me my entire life."

"What are you doing sitting there?"

"Me? I'm searching for my destiny."

"Destiny is not found; it is made."

"How did I get here? And how did you get here?"

"No one knows that. I've been wandering here for centuries."

"What's your name?"

"I have no name. I was found in the trash. After causing a lot of evil in the world, I came here to do my penance. If you saw me in a desert, it wasn't me, just my soul that sometimes wanders sadly and meditatively. My voice is known only by the night, bouncing from rock to rock until it gets lost in the infinite, only to return and cause more evil. Here, alone in the temple, I have no hunger, sorrow, or thirst; I only think about going back where I came from. One day, I dreamed someone would come, and we would switch places. I propose something, young man: you take my broom and other cleaning tools, and ask me for any favor, and I will leave, and you will stay."

"How do we know this will work?"

"It's already written."

"Alright," said Toribio, "take water from that fountain to my brother, but I don't know if he's still alive."

"Don't worry. Here, a second is a thousand years, and a thousand years a second. Your brother is surely alive."

The one-eyed man returned to the Arizona desert to bring water to Matthias. Matthias was desperately drinking the water and trying to wake his brother Toribio, who had fallen asleep forever. Matthias's cries turned into screams that echoed across the desert:

"Brother, don't leave me alone, please! My dear brother, don't leave me!"

The evening news reported: "Fourteen undocumented immigrants found; only two survived." The images showed the faces of Matthias and the one-eyed man on television as they were transported to a hospital. In a far-off place, Toribio was cleaning a large marble statue.

"I hope my brother is okay and that the one-eyed man didn't fail me," he said to himself, "even if I spend my whole life here. I hope he didn't die of dehydration, even if I stay trapped in this immense cell the size of the world for all eternity."

The Mortician

LUCAS MONTERO, THE TOWN MORTICIAN, WAS AN ENIGMATIC FIGURE. Though his profession was grim, he found a peculiar sense of dignity in serving society with care. Known for his unpleasant smell and somber conversations, he was avoided by nearly everyone. After long nights at work, he would stop by a local tavern for a dark beer, his only moment of respite from the isolation that surrounded him.

He lived in seclusion, his life marked by monotony and solitude. On weekends, he tended to his small dog, his only companion, and rested as if he were a laborer.

Gradually, he began to notice unfamiliar items appearing in his home: scythes used for harvesting wheat, farmers' clothing, and various farming tools. "Who is bringing all these tools to my house when I'm not here?" he wondered. His nights were filled with dreams of pastoral scenes—rivers, bridges, railways, and a distant family whose faces remained blurry. This unsettled him, as he couldn't make sense of it.

He continued his peculiar existence, devoid of ideals or aspirations for the future. He was just another person who could have been a shoemaker or baker, but instead, fate had cast him as a mortician. One day, he fell asleep dreaming of pastoral landscapes and awoke in a small rural town. At first, he thought it was just a dream, but hunger and thirst soon proved otherwise. It was at the train station that children jolted him from his daze.

"Daddy, Daddy, don't leave, my mom is sick."

"But I'm not your dad!"

They nearly dragged him to a shabby house where a woman lay on a makeshift bed.

"Darling, why are you wearing such fine clothes?"

"I don't know; it seems I'm losing my mind."

"Daddy, Daddy, we're hungry, but we know you don't have money."

"What do you mean I don't? Here, I have a thousand dollars."

"John, where did you get that money?" the woman asked.

"My name isn't John; it's Lucas."

"Why have you been gone so long?"

"With this money, go buy some food and bring the doctor," he instructed the children.

After a conversation with the man, the doctor remarked:

"Look, John, your stories are quite fantastical. The only oddity is why you disappear every three months and return with large sums of money. One of these nights, you'll vanish again, and we'll search everywhere, only to find you at the train stations."

"Doctor, my name is Lucas, and in another city, I'm a mortician."

"Look, John, you're not schizophrenic, but your case is very interesting."

As night gave way to morning, bringing a sense of calm, Lucas awoke in the city. He found himself unshaven, dressed in farmers' overalls, and without any money. Clutched in his hand were pictures of three children and a beautiful wife.

"I need to see a good doctor!"

His life fell back into its ordinary, sordid routine, tending to corpses and charging exorbitant fees. Occasionally, he'd wake up with pictures of the three children—now older—and think, "If I visited them, I hope I brought them money."

In the town, he remained despised, except by his little dog. Each morning, he read the newspaper and watered his plants. One day, feeling ill, he collapsed among the corpses. Meanwhile, somewhere else, someone was waking him at the train station.

"Daddy, Daddy, we were waiting for you; Mom is also waiting for you."

"Children, in the last photograph, you looked older."

"Daddy, you left three months ago."

"Children, I promise I won't disappear again."

When he arrived, he found a mansion and a thriving hay business.

"Whose property is this?"

"Ours; it's from the money you've been sending us."

"Me? But how?"

He then thought, "Better not to ask; let's just enjoy our life here."

The Unburied Woman

|

AS A BOXING PROMOTER, YOU GET USED TO TRAVELING TO DIFFERENT places in search of new talent. In December of 1999, just before the 20th century ended, I went to Mexico City to scout fighters from Tepito, the rough neighborhood known for producing the country's best boxers. These fighters are always a spectacle, willing to lay down their lives in the ring—true titans of boxing.

In Mexico City, I was warmly welcomed by the press, promoters, and old friends—a crowd of beautiful people surrounding me, celebrating my presence. We dined at Miralto, atop the Latin American Tower, enjoying exotic dishes and intoxicatingly sweet drinks.

Between sips, I noticed her. She was alone, dressed in gray, taking photographs. Our eyes met, and we struck up a conversation. I soon realized she was a woman who never smiled. I invited her out, and she agreed. The next day, we strolled through Chapultepec Park and visited the Tamayo Museum. I had a great time with my new friend. She was beautiful, but her somberness was enigmatic. At times, I wondered if she had deep psychological issues because she sometimes seemed almost lifeless.

II

The promoter paused several times during his story, swallowing small white pills from a case and washing them down with water. Despite his calm demeanor, the compulsive sideways movement of his eyes—like he feared an attack—led the Jesuit priest beside him to think the man might need psychiatric help. However, in his long career as an exorcist, the priest had encountered much worse cases of mental dysfunction. The promoter resumed his tale.

III

When we left the museum, a cold, heavy winter rain caught us by surprise. I laughed, but my companion became anxious and fainted. I caught her just in time and carried her to the car I had rented the day before, placing her in the back seat before driving to my hotel. I carried her up to my room because she hadn't regained consciousness. To my surprise, she was unusually light. Feeling uneasy, I decided to check her wallet but found no identification, no money, no credit cards, no addresses—nothing to tell me who she was. The only thing I knew was her name: Nubia. But I didn't know her last name. I would have to wait for her to wake up so I could call a taxi and send her home.

The night passed. By ten the next morning, I shook her, spoke to her, even tried to revive her, but she was cold and noticeably stiff. She was dead! I nearly had a heart attack—I had spent the night with a corpse. Who could I call? What should I do? People would think I was crazy or that I'd murdered her. I don't know what happened that day, but as night fell, I loaded her into the car and drove her to a park. I placed her on a bench, hoping someone would find her in the morning and the police would report her as dead. Back at the hotel, I informed the front desk that I'd be checking out the following night. My plan was to catch the "Owl" flight—uncomfortable but reliable.

However, at three in the morning, I woke up feeling restless, though I couldn't pinpoint why. I turned on the light, and my heart nearly leapt out of my chest. There she was, standing at the foot of my bed—motionless, her eyes wide open. I don't know how I dared to touch her, but yes, she was dead! Her clothes and hair were wet, her shoes muddy, as if she had walked a long distance. This time, I didn't hesitate. I carried her back to the car and drove out into the night.

A few blocks away, I found a rundown funeral home offering twenty-four-hour services. I explained my dreadful situation, handed over a thick wad of cash, and requested a false death certificate to have her buried. While the paperwork was being processed, the embalmers prepared her for the coffin. Despite my terror, I decided to stay in that house of sorrow rather than leave at that hour. I struck up a conversation with the embalmers, who, with cheerful laughter and little solemnity, busied themselves with the grim task of making the dead appear peaceful in their coffins. Nubia was becoming so beautiful! She looked like a goddess from Greek mythology. Her face radiated peace and serenity, a calm that only death could grant. It was nothing like the storm outside, where the terrible wind was lifting leaves and forming gusts of rain that made visibility impossible.

IV

The protagonist, a boxing promoter and worldly man, finds himself in a bizarre situation. He meets a beautiful woman who, when caught in the rain, faints and subsequently dies. He decides to bury her to end two days of nightmares.

V

At the funeral home, the arrangements were made, but with the rain still falling, I decided to stay in the parlor until the weather improved. Everyone had left except for an old janitor and me. He disappeared into the old mansion that housed the funeral home, and I fell asleep near a large fireplace. In my dreams, I began to imagine what death would be like—the end of our days when the illusion can no longer fly and remains static, like a dead flower losing its petals of hope. I envisioned death as beautiful: an awakening full of flowers, hymns of praise, crowds dressed in white, a legion of angels with curly blonde hair and pearly skin, blowing their magnificent trumpets. You, my Greek goddess, are on that ship of death, crossing hostile seas, drifting away from me forever. You were almost mine before, but now you are the wind.

A few drops of dew woke me in a forgotten garden. How did I get there? I don't know, but I immediately returned to the hotel to settle my affairs and disappear as soon as possible. Before I left, I called the funeral home, where they told me they had found Nubia sitting on the old sofa near the fireplace after I had left. I begged them to bury her immediately and to seal the coffin shut.

VI

Two weeks after returning to California, I read in *Excelsior* that I was being sought in Mexico for prosecution. They had discovered the false death certificate and accused me of burying a photographer alive. According to what I learned from other sources, Nubia suffered from cataleptic attacks, a rare disorder where the heart beats only once a minute, giving the appearance of death, although the body doesn't decompose. Indian masters use this practice, called *actus mortis*, in their yoga exercises. The photographer had been found in her coffin, face down, her face disfigured by terror. They say she managed to live for several hours, buried alive, until horror and despair drove her mad, and she died of asphyxiation.

Unable to get her out of my mind and imagining her everywhere, suffocating in a coffin, I decided to seek refuge indefinitely in a church. During the Middle Ages, those pursued by demons always sought a safe and neutral place, usually a sanctuary, where their tormentors couldn't reach them.

One night, on Halloween, after leaving my refuge to return home, I watched through the window as people, young and old, already in costume, roamed the streets. People choose the costume their subconscious suggests: my neighbor, for example, a beautiful woman, was dressed as a witch, laughing and joking, unaware that she was exactly what she portrayed—a witch.

Suddenly, in front of my house, an old carriage appeared, pulled by four black horses, carrying four hooded figures escorting a coffin. I thought to myself that this was the most original prank I had ever seen, but as I got closer to take a look, I was shocked to see the photographer inside! Through the glass, I saw her face, ravaged by her own nails.

Gripped by panic and desperation, more terrified than ever, I ran back to my sanctuary, where I hope my torment will eventually end—if not, I think I'm going to lose my mind.

The Sniper

I HAD ENLISTED IN THE U.S. ARMY TO FIGHT IN THE GULF WAR. I TOOK out over 300 enemy soldiers, though only 189 deaths were confirmed. But one day, my luck ran out, and I stepped on a landmine, nearly costing me my life. Caught between unconsciousness, agony, and death, the doctors gave me only hours to live; I was dying.

That fateful night, I awaited "the Grim Reaper." I also expected those ominous black-clad figures to arrive, but they never came. Instead, two tall, slender angels in white robes appeared, their eyes unblinking. They offered me one last wish.

"Aurelio, ask us for anything—except to survive," they said.

"What I want is to see my mother as a young girl of fifteen, before she gave birth to me," I replied, clinging to life.

"Granted! But don't speak to her or look directly at her, as she might suspect you know her and could go into shock. Time is of the essence! Tonight, near her home in Parral, Chihuahua, on Matamoros Street, you can see her when she leaves the bakery. Just wait outside, and you'll see her about four years before she brought you into this world."

I did as I was told and waited in anticipation.

There she was! She walked by in her modest but neatly pressed dress, and her old shoes polished. She was eating a piece of bread known as "turtle shells," though in Parral they also call them "guayabas," and in Ciudad Juárez, "sponges."

When she saw me, she paused, as if I looked familiar. I had to turn toward a wall and cover my face with a red handkerchief to hide my tears; the sight was overwhelming.

By the grace of the Creator, I survived and healed. The next morning, I was out of danger, though without legs from the knees down. Over time, I learned to walk with titanium prosthetic legs. I became a marksmanship instructor for the Army, teaching new recruits at military facilities like Fort Bliss in El Paso, Texas, and Fort Lewis in Washington state.

Throughout my life, I had many adventures and romances, but the memory of seeing my fifteen-year-old mother remains etched in my soul forever.

Echoes of the Lagoon

HER NAME EVOKED IMAGES OF RIVERS AND MUD. HER NAME WAS a song. Maribel del Carmen disembarked when the wagon reached the 'Y'; evening was beginning to fall.

"Thank you, Mr. Pantaleon."

"It's nothing, girl. Hurry up, your parents must be worried."

She walked home, passing the Saint Hyacinth estate, now in ruins. The crumbling buildings, coupled with the persistent smell of mildew, brought painful memories of her sister Severine. Her grandmother had always said that Severine had died of typhus during the Revolution, a virulent disease that had ravaged the region for years.

A few days after Severine's burial, something strange happened. She appeared in one of the stables, dressed in a black gown with a shawl covering her head. Maribel del Carmen couldn't shake the feeling that this was no place for wandering, especially at night.

As autumn arrived, the north wind blew with a cold, relentless breeze. Maribel hurried past, her steps quickened by the fear of Jin Chan, a mythical creature said to rise from the waters to hunt mortals. Rumors of this beast haunted her thoughts, even as she dismissed them as village tales.

The truth was, for months, someone had been watching her—obsessed by the beauty that had captivated men since she was sixteen.

Maribel thought to herself, *Once I get to the ranch and have a hot corn-flour drink, I'll feel better*. But suddenly, everything blurred. The coolness of the grass against her face was the only thing she could grasp. She couldn't understand what was happening—her feet refused to move forward. The night deepened, casting shadows over the withered trees. Her body felt lifeless, and she imagined her parents waiting for her. It seemed like a dream—lying there, senseless, feeling the cold seep into her bones, as though she were already submerged in the lagoon's water.

If that's the case, she thought, *I don't want to see the green sludge. The Jin Chan might rise from it like a toad from the river.*

She couldn't control the urge to cry. She didn't know how long she had been in this state, but she knew her parents must be worried. She prayed silently that she wouldn't drown—if only to spare them the pain.

Sometimes, I see small fish with timid faces and cold mouths surrounding me, kissing my skin everywhere. One day, after what felt like an eternity, I managed to leave the water, desperate to find my home. But everything was shrouded in fog, and I couldn't locate it. Panic set in, and I returned to the lagoon, only to lose my way again.

I stumbled upon the estate where I saw Severine. She threw rocks at me, her voice harsh: "Damn dead girl! Go scare someone else; this is where I do my penance! Don't you know? Philip, my brother-in-law, killed the fool for stealing apples, and I'm serving penance for him."

Her toothless mouth sent a chill down my spine, and I told myself, I'm not dead.

I sat on a rock, crying and confused, weeping into the night, probably until about four in the morning. The moon had shifted in the sky when Mr. Pantaleon finally spoke to me.

"Girl, wake up!"

"Mr. Pantaleon, I'm so glad to see you. I'm very scared; please take me home."

"Carmelita, I can't take you where I'm going. I can only tell you that your parents are waiting for you over those hills where the sun sets in the afternoon."

Mr. Pantaleon, the old coachman, swatted at fireflies with his tattered hat before vanishing into the mist. I tried to find him, but my search was in vain. In the morning, the treacherous wind picked me up like a speck of dust. To where? I don't know.

***

At a rundown bar on the U.S.-Mexico border, two women of ill repute exchanged words.

"How was your night, sis?"

"Terrible, no clients."

"Hey, I'm really worried. I've been dreaming for months about drowning in a lake but never actually drowning. What could it mean?"

"Who knows? Stop thinking nonsense. Look... there are some guys over there; let's go see them."

"Alright, panther."

Time passed, and Olivia's dreams persisted. She used her nighttime job as an excuse to drink and drown her sorrows with clients, hoping that getting drunk would ease her conscience—but it never did. One evening, a country taxi driver, who had quietly listened to her complaints, offered her some advice.

"Listen, sweetheart, even if you've tried all the remedies, you've got to keep searching for another way. My old man, God rest his soul, always said you've got to grab the bull by the horns. So tell me, where are you having these dreams? Which city?"

"In a lagoon."

"Yes, but which city?"

"Near the 'Y', beside Saint Barbara."

"You must be kidding! It's south of the state; that's where everything you're looking for is. Ask for a week off, and you'll be free of any curses."

***

Olivia was driven to the lagoon by the taxi driver.

"Are you sure you're not from here?"

"No, I've told you, I'm from the Northern Passage."

"Alright, there's your lagoon. Just don't stay too long; at night, you might hear the ghost of a little girl crying."

"Thank you, I won't stay long."

She walked through the places she had seen in her dreams and reached the shore of the lake, where a sudden realization struck her. The landscape seemed hauntingly familiar, as if the mist and moonlight had etched it into her very soul, drawing her into a past she couldn't remember but felt deeply connected to. She lay in the grass, crying over the miserable life she had, yearning for an uncomplicated past. In her mind, she saw herself as a sad little girl—her tiny feet barely touching the ground, her round face rosy like an apple, pretending to be a woman. Her father had bought her a shawl and a pair of pretty sandals. She spent the entire afternoon crying uncontrollably until she finally returned to where the taxi driver was waiting for her.

"Maribel del Carmen, it's getting dark," the taxi driver said, bringing her back to reality.

"No, sir, my name is Olivia."

"Sorry, my father, God rest his soul, used to talk a lot about 'the girl from the lake,' and you remind me of her."

As he spoke, a faint whisper of recognition seemed to linger between them, a spectral echo connecting Olivia's present with Maribel del Carmen's past. No one noticed anything unusual as the taxi driver took her to the bus station. Olivia returned to her destination, reunited with a profound peace in her soul.

The Cemetery of
the Unborn

AFTER SURVIVING THE ARMED CONFLICT OF THE MEXICAN REVOLUTION and the Spanish flu epidemic of 1918, my paternal grandmother, Manuela Rodríguez—affectionately known as Ala—died in 1982, at nearly eighty-four years old. Despite her passing, my grandmother seemed unable to leave me, following me day and night. At any hour of the night, I would see her praying with her rosary, always facing away from me. She always seemed to be trying to tell me something, but only incoherent mumblings came out of her mouth.

At first, her presence was terrifying, but over time it became almost normal. My hair would only stand on end when she passed effortlessly through walls. In life, she had told me how she once saw her sister walking out of a stable, a shawl draped solemnly over her head and shoulders, her gaze distant. This happened just days after her sister died.

Sometimes, she would visit me in my dreams and say, "I shouldn't have died yet," and then leave. She was always floating, never quite touching the ground.

One day, she said to me:

"Your house is filled with bad energy. I suffered from an evil spirit back at the ranch in El Hormiguero. Sometimes it would lift me out of bed, until a Jesuit priest taught me a prayer: 'Jesus, I see enemies that you need to drive away; they want the blood from my veins, but I won't give it to them. Blessed be the Most Holy Sacrament of the Altar.' I repeated that prayer constantly until the creature that would come out of the wall and wake me finally disappeared."

Then, one night, I decided to follow her down the unknown streets of life.

"Grandma, where are we going?" I asked.

"I'll show you, but don't make any noise," she replied. "We're going to the cemetery of the unborn children. Look at their glass coffins—little pink babies with angelic faces. That section over there is for the girls, and here is where the most awaited ones are, those who never came to be born. Look at them in their christening gowns, some still waiting for the most longed-for embrace from their mothers. This is my eternal task. This is as far as you can go with me. Once you cross over to that side, there's no turning back."

"Goodbye, Grandma," I said, my voice trembling.

"Goodbye, my son. The Almighty still has many new beginnings in store for you."

I woke up to a new day, my heart filled with renewed hope.

The Return

ONE AFTERNOON, AFTER RETURNING FROM A BALL GAME IN MY favorite car, I was driving between Hope and Life streets in California when everything went blank. The last thing I remember was seeing the street signs before I lost consciousness. When I woke up, I found myself in the branches of a tall tree. The growls of a fierce animal echoed around me, and I quickly climbed higher, my heart pounding. I wasn't just scared—I was petrified. For days, I clung to the tree, numb to hunger and thirst, questioning whether I was dead. Desperate for answers, I prayed to the Creator.

One morning, I descended from the tree and, to my surprise, found my favorite car waiting for me. I climbed into my Cadillac, but my perception of time had shifted. No longer did I think in terms of days; everything felt like fleeting moments. During one of my prayers, I asked to see my dog, and the Creator answered. Time bent, and suddenly, there he was— my dog, Duke, scratching at the car window. I opened the door, and his presence brought me a deep sense of peace.

Nights were filled with anxiety, and I clung to Duke even more tightly. I had lost him in my youth, but now, in my golden years, he had returned to me.

In a hospital, some nurses spoke in hushed tones: "This man who came in a few weeks ago thinks his pillow is his dog. He hugs it with such fervor and affection. God help those who lose their sanity."

Night fell over the city. It was December, and snow blanketed Ventura, California. While children eagerly awaited their Christmas toys, one man, in his dreams, continued to climb up and down a tree and hide in the back of his car.

Whirlwind of Emotions

I **WAS SEMI-RETIRED WHEN I BEGAN WORKING AT A HOSPITAL IN SAN** Gabriel County, California. Occasionally, I was asked to assist the staff in transporting bodies to the morgue, whether they were adults or infants. Each time, I said my farewells in my own way.

I worked the evening shift, from three in the afternoon to eleven at night, and I was content. My children had their own families, and I lived alone in a small apartment with my two pets for company.

As a security guard, I maintained a life of strict discipline. One afternoon, I crossed a bridge where a lush river once flowed; now, it was reduced to a meager trickle. I can't recall if it was in La Puente, Pomona, or El Monte—names that harked back to the days when the Spanish ruled Alta California.

That evening, at the hospital, I was called to help transport a body to the morgue. I arrived at the ominous Room 13 on the first floor, where the staff was already placing the body into a thick black plastic bag. I bid farewell in my own manner—pressing my cross with my left hand as a gesture of my Christian faith while clutching my pagan amulet, a gift from a Peruvian indigenous woman, in my right hand. Now in my senior years, I refused to let despair take hold of me. I thanked the Almighty for granting me a fulfilling work life.

Once in the morgue, we placed the body on a shelf, and I stayed behind to offer my prayers. But as night turned into morning, something unusual began to unfold. I started hearing voices all around me: *"I shouldn't have died yet!" and "What will happen to my children?"* The atmosphere grew eerie, and I realized I couldn't find the way out. All I could see were kaleidoscopic lights and endless tunnels of brilliance while haunting Gregorian chants echoed around me.

In my mind, I revisited my childhood and relived my entire life in vivid detail. I felt caught in a whirlwind of emotions—a surreal mixture of nostalgia, fear, and resignation.

I was missing from my post for over a day, and I feared I might lose my job. Then I felt the gentle touch of an elderly man's hand on my shoulder. His voice, soothing and firm, broke through my confusion:

"Stop struggling; you're in a better place now. Rest peacefully, my child. Let go of the day's labor and embrace tranquility. Your troubles are behind you, and you need not worry any longer."

The Cantina Behind the Cathedral

EVERY TIME I VISIT THE CASINOS IN CIUDAD JUÁREZ, CHIHUAHUA, I stay at a centrally located hotel. I spend a few days there before heading to conferences in the southern part of the country. One night, unable to sleep, I left the hotel to shake off my restlessness. In that hostile city, where crime and danger lurked around every corner, everyone was both a victim and a perpetrator. From the shadows of an alley, three individuals started following me, oblivious to the presence of nearby security agents. I was almost running. Behind the cathedral, I spotted a cantina-pool hall with its lights on. I entered, feeling a bit nervous. In the center of the place stood a large, bald man with a dark complexion. He greeted me with a reassuring comment:

"You'll be safe here," he said.

"How do you know?" I asked, intrigued.

He responded with another question:

"Do you see the monitor in front of you? Those are the three who were following you, hiding."

"Do you want to play pool?" he asked again.

"Sure," I replied.

"I knew you'd say yes," he remarked.

"I can size people up in seconds," I warned him. "With you, it's better to play cards."

"Do you see that room at the back?" he continued. "They need a player there; there's an empty chair."

"Thanks."

"You can play at night; the game is poker. We start with five hundred." He rubbed his wallet, revealing ten thousand U.S. dollars. "Alright, here are my five hundred and five thousand more," he said defiantly. Before looking at the cards, he was dealt two kings and three twos. "I need three more cards and another thousand," he insisted.

We played all night, losing track of time. Three days and nights passed. It was strange that I never saw the faces of the other players.

"Gentlemen, I'm leaving," I declared. "I'll collect my money because I want to go back to the hotel and freshen up. We'll continue tomorrow."

The bald man in charge said:

"We've already sent for your clothes and suitcase from the hotel."

"But..."

"Stay here a few more days and continue the game tomorrow after you rest. Go up the stairs to the last room; a good bed awaits you."

In the morning, I realized I had slept for two consecutive days. A woman with her face covered approached me to inform me that breakfast was served downstairs. Everything was perfect, except for the breakfast, which always came with kidneys. Why? Different people interacted at the table where we played cards. New faces.

"What happened to the people from last week?" I asked.

"We turn the losers into smoke."

Nobody said anything, and I kept playing. On the third day, I retired to sleep and accidentally entered another room, where I saw about twenty or thirty jars covered with small cloths. How strange! As I left, the woman was waiting for me.

"That's not your room."

"Excuse me, what are those jars for?"

"They contain the souls of the losers."

"And the thin cloths, what are they for?"

"To keep them from escaping. Souls are loyal; if you tell them to stay, they will."

"What am I doing here?" I asked.

"You, until you win everything, will stay. If you lose, you'll bet your soul and stay here."

"I wagered my freedom, and here I am."

I kept winning enormous amounts of money until one day I said:

"All or nothing..." and lost close to seven hundred fifty million pesos. The bald man said:

"Your soul for everything; the place and the money."

Knowing I was about to lose, I said:

"Thanks, but no, I'm leaving worse off than when I arrived."

A door opened, and a clear, fresh morning greeted me. I headed to the hotel. After walking more than two blocks, I realized I'd forgotten the hotel's location. When I returned, I found that the cantina, the door—everything had disappeared! I stopped at El Madrid, a restaurant where my Uncle Poncho worked in the sixties. As I looked at myself in the mirror, I was disturbed by the white color of my hair.

"God gave me one more chance," I told myself. "Blessed be His name."

The Road of Evil

THAT NIGHT, I CROSSED THE BORDER AT THE PUENTE LIBRE IN EL PASO, Texas. I headed to a warehouse to purchase goods for smuggling into Mexico. After loading the trailer truck with electronics and miscellaneous items, I set off for Mexico to resell them.

On my way to the Rio Grande Valley, late at night, I took the wrong highway and ended up in Arkansas. Suddenly, a dark cloud impaired my visibility. Strangely, the cloud seemed to cut through the fog. Once I passed through its density, I felt like I had crossed a time barrier and found myself in a neighborhood with a mostly white population.

"Am I somehow back in 1930, when discrimination and racism were rampant?" I wondered.

I stopped to refuel as the truck was barely moving on the reserve tank. Curiosity struck me when I noticed people looking at me suspiciously. Despite being a forty-year-old man, everyone who approached me called me "boy."

On my way back to Texas, I witnessed two lynchings. I thought the victims were Mexicans, but no—they were Black men. I felt the harsh sting of racism through those brutal and irrational attacks.

When I finally returned to El Paso, after more than twenty hours of driving, I crossed into Mexico. The customs officer asked for a "bribe," supposedly "for coffee." It wasn't that I didn't want to grease his palm; I was paralyzed by the horror of what I had seen earlier. To calm him, I offered a thousand pesos, but he didn't take the bait. I tried to increase the amount, but with a perplexed look, he confiscated my goods to end the attempted bribe.

When my father, Mr. Lara—author of the song "The Roan Horse" and owner of the bar *The Dinosaurs' Watering Hole*—found out, he scolded me, upset:

"How could you be so stupid, you son of a gun! What were you thinking when he asked for 'coffee'? Did you really think he'd accept sugar cubes? We lost a shipment worth a hundred thousand pesos! Now I have to deal with another bastard who'll accept my terms."

"Father, I have one question: What color am I?"

With a hint of irony, he replied:

"Pale! You've been looking sickly ever since you got back. Was the trip that rough on you?"

"Father, it won't happen again," I promised.

"Go get some rest," he said. "I hope you didn't take the shortcut they call 'The Road of Evil'; many never return."

That was exactly the wrong route I took in an attempt to speed up the journey. You get what you pay for; I'll handle the rest another time.

Don't Leave the Hotel

WHETHER IT WAS FORTUNE OR MISFORTUNE, I WON A LITERARY AWARD that required me to travel to Chicago's south side to accept it. Everyone advised me—no, warned me, "Don't leave the hotel."

"Is it a bad area?" I asked.

"No, it's an area abandoned by God."

The cab driver, an eccentric man with the accent of the Lesser Antilles, laughed as he echoed the caution: "Man, don't go out at night."

"Okay," I said, though unease began to creep in.

On Saturday evening, the auditorium buzzed with activity as many recipients accepted their awards. By 8:30, the crowd had vanished, leaving the cab driver waiting for me outside.

"Man, what time are you leaving?" he asked.

"Tomorrow at five in the morning," I replied.

"I'll be here at five, no worries," he said cheerfully.

I thought, *People here are really helpful.*

Back at the hotel, thirst struck me. I headed to the bar, but it was already closed—so was the restaurant. I recalled the warnings: *Don't leave the hotel.* But I stepped outside anyway.

The streets were desolate, not a soul in sight. There wasn't a single place open to grab a drink or a bite to eat. I returned to the hotel, only to find all the entrances locked. I tried every door, called the front desk, pounded on the glass—but nothing.

Frustrated and uneasy, I wandered to the parking lot. Out of nowhere, twenty frogmen emerged from a nearby manhole, their movements eerie and otherworldly. And then, the worst appeared: the Seven Deadly Sins.

Gluttony was the most grotesque of all—a dark-skinned woman, immense and hunched, with a bulbous mass on her back oozing a green, translucent liquid that resembled pus. I caught glimpses of the others—wrath, lust, sloth—and I managed to evade them by hiding in the shadows.

An hour passed before I finally found a way back into the hotel.

The next morning, I took the first flight back to California. If I ever win another award, they can mail it to me. I'm done with big cities steeped in corruption and shadows.

Sometimes, I think we live in two parallel worlds: one visible, the other hidden. Certain people see ghostly creatures; others spot goblins slipping through cracks in the walls. Not everyone perceives them.

What do we know about the invisible world? Nothing. We accept its existence on faith alone.

My grandmother used to tell me stories about strange encounters, mysteries that blurred the line between this world and the next. But those tales are for another time.

The Quagmire

THE WINDOWS OF MY HOUSE BEGAN TO SHUT SLOWLY, ONE BY ONE. I no longer had the will to get out of bed. My mind was overwhelmed with thoughts. I yearned to fill myself with life—feeling it slipping away—but then I saw the windows bricked up and sealed with mortar. I realized that I no longer existed in this world.

One day, I went out to my garden and saw an immense, towering wall erected in front of my house, stretching as far as the eye could see. I wondered how I hadn't noticed hundreds of workers building this enormous barrier.

I went to fetch my dog, who followed me reluctantly. Together, we set out along the wall—a towering structure about thirty feet high that stretched for miles in both directions, north and south. I walked along a narrow path beside it. As we crossed a bridge, my dog barked, growled, and refused to go any further. He stayed behind, unmoving. With a heavy heart, I bid him farewell and continued on alone. On the third day, I came across many strange people along the way. By the roadside, I saw my paternal grandfather, calmly roasting quail over an open flame.

"Grandpa Ofo," I said—using the nickname I had for him as a child because I couldn't pronounce his name, *Rodolfo*—"what are you doing?"

"Just waiting for the world to end, my boy," he replied.

"But Grandpa, you passed away a long time ago."

"You too, my boy. You just haven't realized it yet."

"Not me, Grandpa."

"That's what we all say until we get used to the absence of time, the lack of rules, and the tasteless food. I've been here about six months by mortal reckoning because someone told me you were coming. Doña Juana went ahead, saying she was looking for her sister Seferina. Who knows where she is now."

"But who told you I was coming?"

"A white man who lived near you."

"But Grandpa, you don't speak English."

"On this side, you don't need to know anything. Look, do you see those bandits?"— he pointed to a gang of outlaws hiding behind a tree. "They've been waiting for their victims for months, not realizing that their prey no longer exists and can't see them. They talk among themselves, dressed in their 19th- or 18th-century outfits. Don't worry, I'll help you find your clan, your pack, whatever you want to call it. The hardest part is arriving here with no one to greet you. Those poor lost souls wander around with no one to show them the way. One day, you'll have to wait for your children, and I'll go look for my little sister Maria, whom I took great care of because she was born with only half a spirit. Don't be sad, your mom and dad are on the other side of that orchard. Don't you hear their laughter? This place is still filled with good people. A few slip through the cracks, and a few fools make mistakes. But since no one waits for them, they spend their time pretending to do what they used to do—stealing, lying, killing. The worst ones even do it in the name of the Creator."

"Grandpa, I'm tired, and I think I'm hungry."

"Eat some quail."

"But Grandpa, this tastes like cardboard."

"You'll get used to it. Come on, let's walk until we reach that orchard. Beyond it lies the path of evil; we'll stick to this side. I'll leave you here, don't worry, I have to go back. See those berries? Take a couple to your parents; it's not customary to arrive empty-handed."

"But Grandpa Ofo, I don't want to get lost."

"Don't worry, your heart always points the way. Let it guide you like a golden compass, one that's infallible."

I hugged my grandfather and said, "Grandpa, I know you died of sadness when your family put you in that nursing home, after you had cared for them your whole life, and reached old age."

"My son, that's all forgotten now. There's forgiveness for everything. Follow that path, and you'll find your parents. I'll catch up later; I have to find my little sister Maria and Doña Juana."

I walked away with a heavy heart, plucked a berry, wrapped a few apples in brown paper, and continued along a path illuminated by a light that seemed to come from nowhere, with no sunlight in sight.

Restless Soul

I GOT OFF THE TRAIN, HAVING UNINTENTIONALLY FOLLOWED MY nephew from Catalina Island. The train seemed comfortable, and during one of its climbs and descents, I stepped off to take in the breathtaking scenery. When the train left without me, I didn't bother to chase it. This wasn't the first time I had been left behind; it had happened before, back in 1963 when I was with Alicia, my wife. I asked her:

"Where are we going?"

She replied:

"To the cemetery, to bury you."

Right there, on Independence Street, I got out of the hearse, terrified, and hid in the mine shafts. All my relatives began disappearing from the village, and I followed them. I'm not sure how I ended up in California and eventually made my way to Catalina Island, then to Anacapa, where I now live. I endure the cold and fear, but I survive the harsh weather.

Many cats live on the cliffs in Ventura. I spend my time there with the anxiety and desperation of a restless soul. I swim back to Catalina Island on dark nights. When I dive into the depths and stay underwater for a long time, I worry because I don't want to die, even though I know I can't die twice. The little fish watch me curiously as I swim, until I finally reach the island. There, only the sheep seem to sense my presence, but I drive them away with rocks.

The nights are damp, with a faint reflection in the moonlit rooms. Tomorrow, I'll return to Ventura, to my life, to my beach, to my cliffs.

Seven Years

IARRIVED IN CASAS GRANDES, CHIHUAHUA—NICKNAMED "CHANTES Longos" by the locals—on my way north. My family was waiting for me in Santa Fe, New Mexico. By the time I got there, it was late, and the 'Red Arrow' bus had already left. So, I decided to stay overnight. I grabbed some grilled cheese and flour tortillas from a local spot. The clerk pointed me in the right direction:

"Head to the village. The bus stops across the street before eleven."

I made my way to Las Moras, a place where women offered their company to the highest bidder. A middle-aged woman greeted me with a knowing smile:

"A fortune teller warned me about you: 'With the frost of years on his sideburns and eyes like the sky,' she said. 'I've been expecting you. Come to my room.'"

Entranced by her gaze, I followed her. The next morning, as I ate breakfast, I felt like Ulysses surrounded by enchantresses. That March 1st of 1977 was a day—and a year—to remember. Seven years have passed since then. I didn't take anything with me, nor did I say goodbye. I went straight to the bus station; everything had changed. From there, I journeyed to New Mexico.

Where did those seven years go? I have no idea, nor do I know what became of Las Moras or that woman, Esmeralda.

I offer thanks to the Creator when I think of March 1st—my brother Roberto's birthday—and for waking from that strange spell. Maybe it was all just a dream.

Oblivion

TO FORGET HER, I VENTURED TO OTHER LANDS. I CROSSED THE BORDER at Puente Libre, where new horizons and fresh hopes awaited me. By nightfall, I arrived at the Federal School in the Park—already in ruins. Undeterred, I continued to State School Three. Passing through the apartment complexes, I found it: my old school, weathered but resilient. A place that had withstood a thousand battles, its humble classrooms untouched by time.

The night surprised me. My old friends were there, waiting. We played a game of three-on-three basketball, like we used to. Pepe and Raúl—affectionately called *Burra* and *Chivo*—were on the court with me. We played until the early hours, our game lit by the glow of car headlights encircling the court.

As dawn approached, the game ended, the headlights faded, and the court emptied. My friends left, one by one. Only Pepe remained. He stepped closer to greet me, his voice soft but steady.

"I knew you'd come, Onti. We've waited for you, every moonlit night."

"I didn't know, Pepe," I replied. "I didn't know COVID had taken you."

"Don't tell anyone."

Tears welled up as we embraced, two friends reunited and yet preparing to part once more.

"Until next time," Pepe said. "But hurry to the cemetery—they're burying Patricia, your ex-girlfriend."

"See you later, my friend."

I ran to the cemetery, desperate to see Patricia one last time. But the large black gates were locked.

Her ex-husband stood on the other side, holding a strange phone with three long screens. "She's mine in life and death," he declared. "She left you a message, but I can't find her."

Through the bars, I saw her moving toward a mausoleum, her figure fading into the darkness. I called out, but my voice didn't reach her. I strained to see her, my heart racing, but she was too far away.

The ex-husband's voice rang out behind me, mocking. "In life and in death, it's all good!"

I ignored him, searching desperately. Then, from behind a tree, hidden in the shadows, she appeared. Her gaze met mine—a silent farewell.

An unfulfilled dream, lost to the night. I returned to the border, her memory etched forever in my soul.

The Tragedy

MY GRANDMOTHER USED TO SAY, "YOU GET WHAT YOU PAY FOR."
I lived between Sonora, Mexico, and Arizona, in the United States. Close to retirement, I often took walks through the hills near the border, where many adventurers, seeking to leave their countries behind, ventured into the U.S. hoping for a better life. But instead of finding security and opportunity, many met death in the desert.

One day, I came across a wild pig and decided to adopt it. I took it home and fed it with a baby bottle. Slowly, it grew strong, but as time passed, it became unmanageable, and the situation turned unsustainable. The pig grew to the size of a mountain lion, but far fatter. To me, it was divine, but to the world, it was dangerous. It tore up the grass—not just mine, but my neighbors' as well. It loved to eat not only potatoes but sweet potatoes too, devouring all my crops and those of the neighbors. In the end, I had no choice but to take it to the wilderness and, with great sadness, leave it to its fate.

Time went on, and the crops in Nogales, Arizona, were ravaged by a horde of around five hundred wild pigs or rodents. They destroyed everything. Large bounties were offered for killing wild pigs. Within months, potatoes in Idaho—over a thousand miles away from Nogales—were gnawed and destroyed. A few years later, it was estimated that the herd had grown to two hundred thousand wild pigs. The National Guard, the Navy, and the U.S. Army were called in to eradicate them. Whenever the pigs reached a lake or watering hole, they nearly drained it, taking away the life-giving liquid. Within a few more years, millions of wild pigs were tearing through entire towns, gnawing at trees, and demolishing wooden and concrete structures in cities. They toppled trains and cargo trucks. The damage was immeasurable. Half of North America had disappeared, and Mexico was in ruins. Even Nicaragua wasn't spared by these boars, some of which had grown tusks beside their snouts. The National Guard managed to kill around twenty thousand of these creatures, with their tough skin, muscles, and coarse hair—more like bristles than fur. Their eyes were filled with savage intent.

I decided to set up a refuge at the top of a pine tree in front of my house, where I slept at night; sometimes, I even took naps there. Months passed, and these beasts were undeterred by rifle shots or cannon fire.

One day, I watched helplessly as five hundred pigs destroyed my house. When they noticed me sitting in my favorite tree, they began gnawing at it slowly, trying to instill fear in me. Desperate, I shouted, "Gilbert! Gilbert!" The piglet I had raised appeared an hour later.

I climbed down the ladder I had made and petted Gilbert. He lowered his gaze to the ground as a sign of humility. I spoke to him, telling him to command his companions to stop terrorizing the locals. They were not to blame for me having left him in the wild; it was my own failure to deal with a semi-wild pig. I asked him to speak with the leaders and make peace, so we could all live in harmony.

That afternoon, the pigs disappeared. Through a subterranean cave in the Grand Canyon, they entered an underground world. I kept Gilbert. His enormous hunger was satisfied by the neighbors in Tucson, who brought him tubs of fruits and vegetables. He lived another thirteen years until he finally passed. After that, the world seemed healthier and more peaceful.

My Other Self

DREAMED I WAS DESCENDING THE WINDING HIGHWAY KNOWN as El Caracol. At thirty-three, I was returning to my hometown of Parral, Chihuahua, after two decades away in California. I had left at thirteen, but now I walked the familiar streets, memories tugging at my heels.

I made my way down Independence Street, passing by the towering façade of Saint Joseph Church. But when I reached Merchants Street, everything became a blur.

Suddenly, I saw myself as a teenager—lost, alone, in a town that felt indifferent, even hostile to human beings. Soon, I found myself on Centennial Street, walking along the same wall where, years ago, a man nicknamed "Mastic"—a friend of my Uncle Pepe—had leapt to his death. It was a Saturday when he learned of his best friend's fatal accident, breaking his neck in the fall.

At last, I reached the house at number fifty-four. I knocked, and after a moment, my Aunt Socorro opened the door. From another room, my grandmother emerged, her face etched with both surprise and sorrow.

"What are you doing here, son?" she asked, her voice trembling.

"I came to see my Uncle José," I replied.

"Go to sleep. Tomorrow, people will come to take your uncle to the cemetery. I have two more coffins, if necessary—one for you and one for me."

"Grandma," I said, "I'm not ready yet."

"No one ever is. Our days are numbered, and we all have an expiration date."

I walked to where my uncle's body lay, resting in a coffin. I opened the glass cover and gazed at him—solemn and clean-shaven, his black hair gleaming like a raven's wing. But there was sweat on his forehead, a jarring reminder that he had been dead for three days. They hadn't buried him yet; they were waiting for his mother to arrive from distant lands. The scent of decay clung to the air—an unforgettable smell, raw and inescapable.

The next day, two coffins were lowered into the ground. My grandmother, along with other relatives, wept as they mourned the losses. In one of those coffins, they carried me. I had come back, not to live, but to die beside the uncle I had loved most.

Back in California, I woke from the dream, my heart racing. I sat up and thought: Are we living in parallel worlds? Is my other self on another planet, or perhaps somewhere else on Earth?

No one knows. These are the mysteries of the Almighty. Ever since that night, my recurring dreams have vanished, as though my other self had truly died in a distant land.

The Tunnel and the Train

T HE YEAR 2025 WAS COMING TO AN END. I TOOK THE OPPORTUNITY TO catch the train that would take me to Oregon to visit my son. With Christmas approaching, I had to hurry to get back to California, but not before visiting my favorite spots: the casino, the Blue Boy, the best bars, and the places known for their great hamburgers.

On the way back, the train passed through a tunnel. It lasted about ten or thirteen minutes; I don't remember the exact duration of the trip. When we emerged on the other side, the train stopped for an hour. As a result, I decided to get off and enjoy the fresh mountain air. One of the employees announced that we would have to spend the night there because the tracks a few miles ahead were damaged. Upon disembarking, I felt trapped in a gloomy city. I decided to call it a "metallic city." I wandered through this city filled with solar panels. People stared at me with curiosity. A middle-aged man appeared nearby.

"I'm from Oxnard," I replied to his question.

"How strange," he responded, looking intrigued. "That city no longer exists. It was destroyed about a hundred years ago. I believe it was in the year 2175. What year is it for you?"

"We're in 2525," I replied casually.

"That's not possible," he protested. "I don't know where you're from, but you need to come with me to the police station, where I'm the authority and the magistrate. Let me tell you a story; it seems like you've just woken up from a long sleep... About 400 years ago, the world was full of trash; there were over seven billion people; the prisons were overcrowded with criminals; a Universal Government eliminated all the prisoners of the world. Those who lived on welfare disappeared. The billion people living in extreme poverty in India were also victims of a premeditated extermination. The same Government wiped out one of the four races that produced nothing. Nowadays, quadriplegics can walk: their old spinal cords were replaced with new ones. Occasionally, old spinal cords were repaired. Brain transplants are now common, and we have less than a billion people in the world. Three-quarters of the human race in Africa vanished, and animals began to inhabit areas from Mexico to Argentina. The ones who vanished were people who didn't contribute to society: drug cartels and corrupt politicians. After their disappearance, a quarter of the population lives happier. People now work only three hours a day. You can travel underwater from New York to Madrid in two and a half hours on a supersonic bullet train."

The conversation with that enigmatic figure lulled me to sleep until an authoritative voice brought me back to reality: "Oxnard, California! We will arrive in two minutes." Upon waking, I thought I had had a science fiction dream, but I was back in the year 2025. The most unbelievable part was a postcard that, unbeknownst to me, I had in a pocket of my coat. It displayed an image of a city crowded with buildings of crude, distorted metallic architecture, and the date on the postcard was 2525.

The Guest

ARRIVED IN ROMANIA AT NIGHT AND MADE MY WAY TO THE HOTEL TO shake off the fatigue of the journey; I slept until noon. I was in Bucharest, about one hundred eighty kilometers from the castle of the monster and terror of the Turks: the legendary Dracula. The taxi driver who took me to the medieval fortress was highly superstitious and nervous; he spoke a mix of Romanian and Spanish. I asked him to return for me at five in the afternoon. He dropped me off nearly a kilometer from the castle, and I had to walk the rest of the way.

When I finally arrived, the garden gates were open. In the distance, a slightly ajar door seemed to invite me into what appeared to be a chapel or hall. Inside, there was a table set for about five hundred guests, covered with candles, tapers, and votive lights—there must have been a thousand. It was clear that someone had spent hours lighting them. At the center of the room, there was an opulent coffin draped in elegant black velvet and mahogany. I approached to examine the figure inside. He was of medium height, wearing a silk cape, red on one side and immaculate black on the other. It looked as though he had just passed away, though he had been dead for centuries. The pallor of his face made him appear imposing. He was dressed in a white shirt, a bow tie, and a gold pin topped with a ruby.

I had two intense impulses: to stay for a few hours in front of that indescribable scene or to flee. I chose the latter, just as the gardener was about to close the gates. The taxi driver was already waiting for me, and I thanked him quickly before departing.

Back at the hotel, I prepared for my return trip to the United States. Days later, after I was back home, I received an unexpected surprise: an envelope with no return address, containing a gold pin topped with a blue diamond—a token for attending the celebration. I have no idea how they found my address! This deeply unsettled me. Later, I discovered that I had been the only guest at that strange celebration in the castle.

Gossipy Winds

AFTER SEVERAL MONTHS WORKING AS A SECURITY GUARD AT A CAR dealership, I developed a deep aversion to the job. It became increasingly terrifying, and I felt the need to change my surroundings.

One night, while parked in the company vehicle, a man in a red plaid shirt appeared in front of me. I never saw his face. Later, I learned that he was the ghost of a strawberry picker from the 1940s or 1950s. He had been buried in a small cemetery behind the Guadalupe Chapel, where sacristans, priests, and some church members were interred. It was rumored that the dealership where I worked had been built over that old cemetery.

I moved to Tulare, a town near Visalia, California. Upon arrival, I was completely disoriented by a terrible gale. I couldn't see more than two feet in front of me! I hoped for a downpour or even just a drizzle, but nothing came. I took refuge in a nearby cabin, where an old man kindly offered me shelter.

"Come on in, I was expecting you," he said politely.

"But how did you know I was coming?"

"The gossipy winds revealed your arrival to me. Come in, take refuge from this fierce wind in my kitchen."

"I've never seen such a calamity," I remarked.

"You should get out more often. My name is Matthias, and you are…? In fact, your name isn't important when it comes to doing a good deed. Have something to eat; tomorrow I'll show you my sanctuary."

The next day, in a secret chamber the size of a football field, there were about seven hundred restored images and statues of saints and virgins.

"All the devout bring me their idols; I repair them, touch them up, and send them back to their owners," the man explained. "In that section are the saints with more facial expression. I make them with cemetery soil and human bones to give them a touch of life. When human life ends, that little illusion, soul, or whatever you want to call it, takes refuge in the marrow. People say, 'I pray to this saint because he's miraculous.' They don't realize that I create them. It's better to pray to the heavens and the winds than to a lifeless temple or an inanimate object."

I had to move on to less troubled lands. As soon as I continued my journey, the winds died down, and the air grew eerily calm.

The Bloody Hand

BERNARDO ELIAS WAS THE DRIVER OF THE BUS THAT BECAME THE scene of one of the worst public transportation tragedies. As the bus descended a serpentine slope near Cuernavaca, Morelos, Mexico, the brakes suddenly failed. Although the curves weren't too sharp, the bus overturned. All the passengers died, except for a baby and Bernardo. Those who weren't crushed were left unrecognizable and in agony. In the end, none of the injured passengers survived. The authorities forced Bernardo to take care of the orphaned baby.

After enduring many hardships, he moved to California, United States, where he remarried, taking a Mexican-American woman as his wife. At night, in the hallway of his house that connected all the bedrooms, at the dreaded hour of three in the morning, the unfortunate former driver would get up to check the doors. He would find himself surrounded by about thirty individuals—some burned, others mutilated—all lamenting their horrible fate. Bernardo would retreat to his bedroom with his beloved wife, but almost every night, the same thing happened: he would find mutilated bodies in the bathtub, in the hallway, or even when he was alone in bed.

With visits from a priest and prayers to the Creator, all the ghosts and specters eventually disappeared, except for one thing. Wherever he looked, it was there: if he opened a drawer, he saw a pale, bloodied hand, as if it had been freshly severed. It was a menacing hand that reminded him of his guilt. Sometimes, with his heart pounding, he would get up to check on his son Willy—the baby he had adopted—there it would be, close to the child, who lay peacefully sleeping. The fingers of the hand intertwined with Willy's tiny hands. Bernardo would retreat in horror as he watched the hand move and slide along the wall.

The terror caused by the hand began to fade as Willy grew older and came to understand the tragedy. "Dad, it wasn't your fault!" the teenager would tell him. Little by little, the hand lost its luster, its energy, its vitality, until it finally vanished for good.

By then, Bernardo's mind was no longer sound. He talked to himself. Sometimes, he could be heard saying, "I'll buy you a glove to keep you warm in the winter, my dear hand." Eventually, he was committed to the psychiatric hospital in Camarillo, California. After being discharged, he was often seen wandering the streets of Ventura.

Genetic Games

I HAD JUST MOVED TO A NEW NEIGHBORHOOD IN NORTHERN PHOENIX, Arizona, when I was warned that the house was haunted—filled with goblins and strange, unexplained noises. Rather than feeling dissuaded, I found myself intrigued. A mysterious house posed no challenge for me! I was already used to hearing objects fall and odd sounds coming from corners.

I imagined the previous owners were perhaps inventors or alchemists, searching for the Philosopher's Stone, trying to turn base metals into gold. One day, I ventured down to the basement and stumbled upon a dozen cages that looked like storage rooms but were, in fact, laboratories where they had experimented with animal DNA.

The animals still confined in the cages seemed to possess a high level of intelligence, though they were on the brink of death. The sheep tried to communicate with their eyes, and the pigs made desperate, failed attempts to speak. The only one that actually spoke was a parrot, who chattered coherent words: "Crazy witches, crazy witches!"

Feeling compelled to act, I called the police. Officers arrived, accompanied by experts renowned for their skills. With their advanced techniques, they made all the animals vanish, erasing any evidence as though nothing had ever happened.

Later, I did some research and discovered that the Egyptians, Aztecs, and other ancient civilizations had also experimented with DNA, creating beings like the Cretan Bull, the Feathered Serpent, and other mythical creatures. Sometimes, in my dreams, I hear the voices of the sheep speaking as though they were human.

Eventually, all my notes were stolen, and there was no trace left of what had happened. I couldn't help but wonder, "Are we humans just part of an experiment?" It's anyone's guess.

Parallel Worlds

WHEN I WAS TWENTY-FIVE—MANY MOONS AGO—I GOT DRUNK WITH Álbaro, my old college friend. We drowned ourselves in malt liquor, letting the night slip into a golden haze. Three beers were enough to push me to the edge of oblivion. Yet somehow, I managed to drive toward Frontera—or at least, that's what I thought. In my dazed mind, I was convinced I had landed in Tijuana.

Before reaching Frontera, I stopped at an old restaurant, its lights flickering like a beacon in the night. Two blonde girls—fresh and bright as daisies—stood at the entrance, their smiles warm, almost expectant. They led me inside, handed me a menu. It must have been close to three in the morning, the hour of strange encounters. I marveled at the place—an elegant haven still awake at such an hour.

I ordered everything—medium-rare steak, glistening with juices, resting on a bed of golden potatoes and caramelized onions. Half a bottle of rosé accompanied the feast. The flavors melted on my tongue, rich and perfect. The bill? A mere three dollars and change. "I'm coming back to this place," I told myself.

I kept driving, and suddenly, the world shifted. I wasn't in the past or the future—I had crossed into a Mexico that was the same, yet entirely different. Words were written backward. In every bar and club, the same song played in an endless loop: *La Sirenita (The Little Siren)*—"*One year into marriage… but with a fish's tail…*"

It was a world of brilliance without reason. No one visited doctors; instead, they murmured strange prayers to an unseen force, enslaved by horoscopes and superstition. At the racetrack, the gamblers bet religiously on the same trifecta—one, seven, nine—rarely winning. I placed seven bets and won five; they looked at me as if I wielded divine power.

They were tireless workers yet shackled by absurd beliefs. On the thirteenth of the month, the streets emptied, as if death itself had issued a decree. Beauty and ugliness had switched places, defying all reason. There was no crime, no prisons. The elderly ruled with quiet authority. No one spoke of death—only of "kicking the bucket," nothing more.

I adapted. I dressed like a Mennonite at the university and, without a degree, began teaching common sense. To them, it was as if I were lecturing on quantum physics. My classes were packed. My words carried weight in bars, and in the parks, a silent crowd trailed behind me. I changed my phone number constantly, but the calls never stopped.

I introduced them to new songs—besides *La Sirenita*, they now knew *Cien Años (One Hundred Years)* by Pedro Infante—"*It hurts to the core to know that you've forgotten me…*". But *Mi Matamoros Querido (My Beloved Matamoros)*? That one they knew—but not from Rigo Tovar. In their world, it belonged to *Los Hermanos Prado*.

Then, one afternoon, an eerie fog rolled in, thick and consuming. I tried to escape.

I woke up in my bathroom, my skull splitting with pain. My wife stood over me, arms crossed, eyes sharp as daggers.

"You spent the entire night in the bathtub" she said, her voice laced with contempt. "Drunk out of your mind!"

I opened my mouth to protest, but the words caught in my throat. Had I truly returned? Or was I still lost between worlds, waiting for the fog to take me back?

The Old Man and
the Lighthouse

JOE WILSON WAS RELEASED AFTER THIRTY YEARS IN SAN QUENTIN. He had been imprisoned for armed robbery, illegal possession of weapons, and homicide. Despite his outwardly peaceful demeanor, his lengthy criminal record made it impossible for him to find work. At sixty, he was a burly man with graying temples, a grim expression, and a demeanor that, while cordial, carried an air of danger. The only job he could find was on a remote island in the Lesser Antilles, where a towering lighthouse cast its beam for miles around. A Franco-American company offered him three hundred thousand dollars a year to live there and maintain the isolated lighthouse.

The lighthouse had a dark history—no one who had worked there had ever lasted more than a year. The locals whispered of a curse, but Joe saw it as just another job.

He moved into his new home. It was desolate, but he had grown accustomed to solitude during his prison years. The first three weeks passed, bringing with them ominous clouds; the sea roared with fury, and the waves nearly reached the old lighthouse. The isolation, the storm, the endless sea—all seemed familiar to him, like the walls of a cell.

At night, Joe began experiencing strange hallucinations. The flashes of strange lights, shadowy figures on the cliffs, and voices from the waves didn't trouble him. After thirty years of confinement, he had learned to accept whatever came his way. Life or death, it no longer mattered to him. The loss of family, a wife, or a home—none of it hurt anymore. His dreams had become mere echoes of sanity's final retreat.

He stayed there for two years. Then, without warning, he vanished. The first paycheck of three hundred thousand dollars was collected, but the second was returned, undeliverable due to the lack of a forwarding address. A search was initiated, but no trace of Joe Wilson was ever found on the island.

The records showed that a man named "Joe Wilson" had been incarcerated in San Quentin, California, in the 1930s. He had always dreamed of escape, but he had died there—his body buried, his spirit restless.

What had happened at the lighthouse? No one would ever know.

The Perfect Day

JACINTO WOKE UP IN HIGH SPIRITS. NEWS HAD ARRIVED FROM VARIOUS places informing him that he had inherited estates and other assets from distant relatives—even two exotic dogs from Mongolia! He spent the entire day elated by the news. It was Friday the thirteenth.

The superstition proved wrong, as it turned out to be a day of joy rather than bad luck. He went to the racetrack and won, then headed to the casino and won again. Seven out of ten bets were in his favor. He had to hurry, though, as the day was drawing to a close.

On the street, he played a coin toss with a candy seller and won that as well. He even received a call from the local government, asking him to run for governor, but he ignored it, being a simple man who was made nervous by such matters.

Around eleven at night, with a great fortune in hand, he was waiting for the day to end, and with it, his incredible luck.

That day, the Creator had blessed him, but most importantly, he had lost the woman who was to be his wife. He resolved to give up everything to have her back. That night, in a dream, she spoke to him: "The woman who helped you win at the casino was me. The soul of your beloved was with me. It's hard for you to understand, but I came to see you for a brief moment. We'll meet again soon, Jacinto. Enjoy your fortune."

The Screw

I AWOKE TO FIND MYSELF ASCENDING A STAIRCASE THAT TWISTED AND turned in unnatural, unsettling ways. The people moving upward around me didn't speak or even glance at one another. The same silence shrouded those descending, as if we all carried an unspoken fear. No one dared come close to the edges, terrified of falling into the unknown.

I asked, "Where are we?"

No one had an answer. It seemed as though no one had ever reached either the top or the bottom.

Resigned to the mystery, I sat down to wait. But wait for what? My teacher Celia once spoke of the immortality of the crab, a metaphor suggesting that those lost in their own daydreams live in a state of perpetual, unchanging existence. This place felt eerily similar—a massive, metallic structure resembling a colossal screw or an intricate twist of steel.

One day, exhaustion overwhelmed me, and I sought a moment of rest. In front of me loomed a hotel with what seemed like a thousand doors, each adorned with symbols representing different aspects of life: twenty doors for romantic pursuits, another twenty for one's supposed true calling, others for religion, and even more for personal preferences— whether one is emotionally detached or constantly seeking thrills.

At the heart of this hotel were countless deities, each embodying a fragment of human experience. Because at birth, we have no answers and gain knowledge through the trials and tribulations of life. We stumble upon truths as we falter. We endure humiliations and setbacks while unseen demigods toy with our fates, offering us fleeting successes or imperfect partners. Some find triumph only in their twilight years, or accumulate wealth only to leave it behind for those who never earned or valued it.

The screw of life is a revelation—a reminder that while life may be harsh, it is never truly absurd.

The Deer God

AS A CELEBRATED BUSINESSMAN AND THE RECIPIENT OF THE BEST REAL Estate Agent award for ten consecutive years, my success was measured not in thousands but in millions. I was no longer the young laborer hustling at Mexico City's Central Market but the most sought-after real estate broker in Southern California.

One day, I traveled to Yosemite National Park to meet my friends at Fresh Meadows Camp. They never arrived. Alone and intoxicated, I stumbled upon a watering hole where a herd of deer gathered. Fueled by alcohol and arrogance, I began practicing my aim, targeting the innocent creatures. By the end of the night, I had killed seven deer, each shot through the eyes. Morning came, and with it, the sobering sight of the massacre I had caused. I left the bodies behind, guilt gnawing at me like a restless beast.

That night, I had a dream. A majestic deer with towering antlers appeared in my room, its eyes piercing my soul. It spoke: "For the crime you committed—slaughtering my brothers for sport—you will receive two pieces of news every January: one good and one bad."

And so it began.

On January 13th, the first year, I received a call informing me of an unexpected inheritance—one million dollars from a distant relative. Barely two hours later, another call shattered me: my wife had died in a car accident.

Year after year, the pattern repeated. Good fortune would shine on me in the morning, only to be followed by devastating loss by nightfall. My family was stripped away, one by one, until only my beloved daughter, Anabelle, remained.

Desperation drove me to seek answers. I traveled the world, consulting mystics, fortune-tellers, and spiritual leaders. My Catholic faith took me to France, to the Cathedral of Notre Dame. I recalled Victor Hugo's story of the word *ANANKE*—necessity or fate—etched into the cathedral's towers, inspiring *The Hunchback of Notre-Dame*. But my journey yielded no salvation. Defeated, I returned home.

One day, I encountered a man on the street holding a sign that read: *"Forgive my son, who is to be executed by garrote."* Intrigued, I asked him why he sought forgiveness. He replied, "Only forgiveness can seal a dam, repair a leak, or mend a broken soul."

His words struck a chord. That night, I knelt before the heavens and begged the Deer God for mercy. I poured my heart into the wind, pleading for forgiveness for my selfish crime.

For the first time in years, I slept peacefully. Calm and serenity blanketed my home, and happiness returned to my life. Summers with Anabelle were filled with joy and laughter, unmarred by tragedy. My health remained steadfast, and I lived to a ripe old age, content in the knowledge that I had made amends. When my time came, I ascended to the Heavenly Throne in peace.

The Swallow Man

AT SEVENTY, RAUL RODRIGUEZ, KNOWN AS THE SWALLOW MAN, HAD lived a life full of joys, fond memories, and experiences. But he also carried a dark burden. Time had etched lines on his face, and the shadows of his past loomed larger with each passing day. At eighteen, he enlisted in the Mexican army and fought against Native Americans in northern Mexico and southern Texas.

One fateful day, his regiment arrived at a camp of the Chiricahua natives, only to find the warriors absent. What followed became a haunting tale he would recount to those who dared to listen.

Raul was plagued by recurring dreams: in them, he stood in a tower with four high-powered rifles. He would shoot at everything that moved, racking up over a hundred kills before being taken down himself. Each night, the dream played out the same, like a cursed reel in his mind. These nightmares came most often when he spent his days searching for the fabled mine every prospector in town sought.

"We need to find the vein; with that, we'll get rich, just like the guy who discovered the mine 'La Prieta' in Parral, Chihuahua," he'd tell anyone who joined his futile quest.

Exhausted by his obsessions, Raul often ended his nights at Don Pancho's place. Every purchase came with a shot of the infamous Topitos—small but potent doses of pure alcohol. Just two or three could leave you tipsy, but more would knock you unconscious.

Raul loved to sing songs like "They Took the Cannons to Bachimba" or "The Red-Colored Ones" as he swayed unsteadily on his feet. Then he'd stagger home, laughing and mumbling his favorite line: "I'm going to take a long walk off a short pier."

But one day, the laughter stopped. The town was shaken by the tragic news of Raul's wife, Mariana, passing away. Lost in grief, Raul sought solace at Pancho's tavern.

That night, after a few too many drinks, Raul revealed the truth he had buried for decades. His voice quivered as he recounted what happened at the Chiricahua camp. With no warriors present, the soldiers had turned their weapons on the most vulnerable. They slaughtered not only the elderly but also the children.

Raul sobbed and writhed in anguish, confessing, "Jesus, why didn't you stop my hands? I was the one who had to kill those children. My guilty conscience was dormant, and no one stopped me from doing what I did. I stained my soul with the blood of innocents. Forgive me, Redeeming Father!"

That night, he fell to his knees, crying out, "I killed those little angels, and no one stopped me! We were awarded medals for Great Merit for this action, but I threw mine into the Conchos River." He stumbled home, broken and inconsolable.

Feeling isolated and tormented, Raul sought a way to atone for his sins. In the years that followed, he began taking in street children and orphans, providing them with shelter, food, and a chance at a better life. Thus, The Orphanage was born, a sanctuary built from Raul's sorrow and relentless pursuit of redemption.

The Divine Hunter

I FEEL LIKE I'M DROWNING IN A WARM SEA. A MAN WITH ONLY ONE ARM swims by, catches a fish, and bites off its head in one swift motion. I wake up, sweating, on the same boat taking us to an island from which there is no return. The cooks laugh, revealing their toothless gums, a result of scurvy. Those who spent too much time on ships without eating fruits or vegetables lost their teeth. The captain then spoke to the travelers:

"These cooks have lost their minds from being at sea for so long. If you hear rumors that you won't return, remember that the cooks never came back. Where we're going, you might not return, but what we're doing is for your homeland.

As the ships drew within two hundred meters of the shore, the boats were lowered. They brought eighty Queen's dragons and, with great effort, maneuvered the horses through the dark, cold waters in the early morning shadows. Before dawn, the captain bellowed:

"Anyone who falls behind or does not have a horse will be eaten by demons—ride hard to the fort at The Immaculate Conception!"

The Spanish soldiers moved swiftly, as if sensing their doom. Through the jungle, eerie, inhuman cries echoed.

The captain slowed down and tried to calm the soldiers:

"Load your pistols and muskets and shoot at the trees when I say… Now!"

Not even the gunfire could silence the screams.

"Ride hard! Don't stop until I tell you."

They arrived at the fort by noon, where a hundred soldiers, pale as though they hadn't slept in years, awaited them.

"What's going on? You all look terrified."

One of the soldiers replied:

"You'll see the reality tonight."

The shadows of the night loomed over the fort, its vast steel mesh covering every inch to prevent anyone from entering or leaving. As darkness fell, the jungle seemed to merge with the fortress, and hundreds of demons began scaling its walls, their ascent met with the deafening sound of gunfire. But these sons of Lucifer were so swift that they easily avoided being hit. On rare occasions, they were only slightly wounded. Every night was the same—the infernal beings never relented. When the metal net was breached, one demon would slip in, grab a soldier, and not kill him right away. Instead, they fed him liquids until his body fermented and exploded, feeding on the creatures it birthed; the screams of the condemned were chilling to the bone.

In the mornings, indigenous people brought supplies to the soldiers, but I noticed something strange: why didn't the demons attack them? One day, I spoke with the captain about asking the Indians for help. The Indians refused, citing an ancient pact. One night, the captain tied several Indians outside the fort, and by morning, to everyone's surprise, the Indians were still alive. Their response was:

"We aren't greedy like you. We have someone who can help you."

In the afternoon, they arrived with a blind archer. Everyone laughed at the sight. The blind man calmly asked one of the soldiers to place a coin on his heart. With remarkable speed, he shot an arrow that nearly pierced the coin. When they asked him how he did it, he replied:

"My ears are my eyes; I hear the beating of your heart. I am the 'Divine Archer.' Tonight, I will help you with this plague of infernal beings. One day, you'll realize that you are them, and they are you."

The Divine Archer was a nondescript, short man carrying a quiver full of arrows and a bow that seemed almost childlike. Night fell swiftly, but that night was unlike any other. For hours, no demon approached. The archer requested to be covered with several blankets.

"These devils have already smelled me and know there's an unafraid individual here."

In an instant, the roof was swarming with demons. With the agility of a cat, the archer began to shoot through demon after demon. After losing about ten of their own, the demons began to retreat. The captain ordered the remaining ones to be finished off, and we set out for their lair. The captain commanded me:

"Matthias, go with the blind man into the cave and finish them off."

Inside, it was a grotesque cavern, but deeper within, there were palaces of unmatched beauty. I couldn't find any demons; they had escaped through a series of secret passages beneath the sea. In one of the opulent halls, I found the Divine Archer, an arrow lodged in his heart. Why had he killed himself? As I touched the objects, I felt a power surge through me, an energy like that of a thousand rhinoceroses. My chest expanded, and my arms felt invincible. I knew it was time to leave those rooms.

When I emerged from the cave, ten soldiers threw a net over me and gave me a severe beating.

"Here's one at last; we've caught one."

I tried to scream, but only guttural sounds escaped my throat. When I tried to explain who I was, they beat me. With my hands, I killed two by snapping their necks, then I lost consciousness. When I regained my senses, I realized they were taking me to Spain, bound in chains and covered in filth. My life had become a living nightmare. I felt as if I had been drugged with strange potions. In my cell, I was allowed to rest, but by morning, I easily bent the bars and killed a dozen soldiers and jailers with ruthless efficiency. I almost escaped, but four friars bearing crosses and carrying a liquid that seared my insides stopped me. Along with one of the jailers, they chained me once again and threw me into a dungeon, where I would await judgment by the Holy Inquisition.

Now, here I am, locked in a cell with others who are tortured daily for crimes they did not commit. The priests and bishops take pleasure in watching me kill fellow friars and Christians. It dawned on me that the one place where God is absent is within the walls of the Catholic Church. I will remain here, trapped in this cell with no hope of escape for the rest of my days. They say a demon can endure for a thousand years; may God have mercy on me.

Desert Butterfly

SHE TOLD ME ABOUT THE DESERT REGION OF DURANGO, MEXICO. I'M not sure if it was Mapimí, Tepehuanes, or the Zone of Silence. In 1910, during the armed conflict that sparked the Mexican Revolution, fighters on both sides took whatever they could. My grandmother Manuela would recount how she walked barefoot through those lands, where the burrs and thorns were merciless to the inhabitants. Sometimes, her sister Zeferina lent her sandals so she could go to the river and fetch water.

When the revolutionaries arrived, they seized everything. Without a dowry, marriage became even more difficult. Manuela thought to herself, "I'll end up marrying some scruffy mule driver—someone with a lowly, nearly impoverished trade, just scraping by."

One day, in the midst of a family argument, her mother threw a sandal at her. Manuela fainted. The severity of the impact was unclear, but she was left unconscious. For several hours, she found herself in a desert, flying alongside a swarm of butterflies. They had no voices, but through instinct and a touch of telepathy, they communicated.

It's impossible to explain how, from a place filled with cacti, Manuela was transported to a desert with vast dunes combed by haughty winds, where she became a butterfly soaring through the air, flying without missing a beat. They flew so close to each other, yet never touched.

When she awoke, her father, worried, had taken out a loan to buy her sandals, so she wouldn't hurt herself while fetching water or firewood. He scolded his wife for the incident.

Manuela woke with the morning sun, relieved not to be an ephemeral butterfly. On the porch of her home, she saw a butterfly still alive but struggling, sustained by the warmth of Father Sun.

The Night of Times

IN ONE OF THE CAVES LOCATED ON THE CLIFFS THAT BORDER THE DEAD Sea, near the place where the biblical scrolls were discovered between 1947 and 1956, I came across approximately seven thousand better-preserved papyri from a civilization more advanced than ours. As an amateur archaeologist, I chose not to report the finding. In these papyri, I discovered that the tales of fallen angels were true. Why are they so feared? Because of the harm they have caused humanity. I also confirmed that it was true that beings from the heavens had relations with the daughters of men.

The papyri revealed to me how strange visitors with elongated skulls and slanted eyes had arrived from the Pleiades, how the moon had detached from the earth, causing cataclysms, ice ages, and mini ice ages, and how these visitors, with their metallic ships, had overcome gravity and moved stones weighing thousands of tons to build temples in Greece, Egypt, Teotihuacan, Cusco, and other ancient civilizations.

With an excess of technology, the powers annihilated themselves. Lemuria and Atlantis disappeared, and only the natives of the islands survived. These beings from the first or second civilization had perfected the laser beam and mastered gravity. Interplanetary travel and the transmutation of metals had altered DNA, endowing Neanderthal and Cro-Magnon humans with intelligence but without suppressing their aggression, which can still be seen in boxers, Mixed Martial Arts fighters, law enforcement officers, and prisoners.

I belong to a sect of scientists dedicated to the pursuit of truth, and we continue to study the Dead Sea Scrolls. We have not reported the discovery of the seven thousand papyri to anyone, not even to the Vatican; they would silence us.

Desolation

MY SMALL TOWN WAS DESOLATE, ABANDONED BY THE GODS. A BAND of outlaws had stolen all the country's wealth: mines, banks, oil, and other resources. They handed everything over to their relatives and friends. At night, only a few porters and thieves gathered outside the market, occasionally offering me an orange or a swig of sotol. The porters informed me that the town was becoming a wasteland; everyone had fled to other lands.

Since the closure of the "La Prieta" and "La Esmeralda" mines, there was no way to make a living except as a priest, a thief, or a white slave trader. The latter was difficult, though, as there weren't enough people left, and those who remained were armed with anything they could find, even a corkscrew. Next to the market stood Saint Joseph's Church, where, at night, about twenty women dressed in black resembled a convention of crows as they prayed for the dead.

I wondered, "How did we get here?" I remembered the late sixties when the town's old baseball stadium hosted the fair. What joy there was! Cockfights, card games, even the roulette wheel, and that game tinged with racism—"Hit the Darky." If you hit him with a rubber ball, the crowd would be drenched in water.

There were no more railroads, no more integrity. Nowadays, all that's left is desolation, corrupt mayors, and white-collar thieves. As Voltaire said, "To know a people, you must visit their prisons." One moonlit night, I left for the Borderland... what times those were!

The Russian Theater

ALL MY LIFE, I DREAMED OF BEING A STAGE ACTOR—PERFORMING under the spotlight, becoming Cervantes' Don Quixote or Shakespeare's Hamlet. But it never happened.

As I grew older, I lost my wife, and my three children left the nest. At eighty, I found myself anchored on the coast of California, waiting for death with its gleaming, silver, and ferocious scythe. I awaited it eagerly, with a sense of joy. My grandmother used to say, "We're just passing through, after all."

When the hospital bathroom tiles changed color from yellow to blue, they assigned me an austere nurse. She was strict, unsmiling, and perhaps, to some, unattractive. In my thoughts, I would sometimes chuckle, thinking, "She just needs to shave her mustache." My family insisted on taking me home, worried I was losing my mind. But the truth was, I was simply tired of arguing.

One quiet night, as the wind hummed through the window, a pink, blue, and yellow dragonfly woke me up. Its wings shimmered with an otherworldly glow.

"Don't open the closet; we have a surprise for you," it whispered in a voice that was both melodic and commanding.

"Fine, I won't tell the nurse," I replied with a mischievous grin. "Otherwise, she'll send me to the psych ward!"

For days, I resisted the temptation to open the closet door, counting each moment until March 1st. I remember the date because it's my brother Roberto's birthday.

At midnight, the closet door creaked open on its own. Inside was a tiny theater, bathed in warm, golden light. To my astonishment, it showcased the famous Russian dancers Rudolf Nureyev and Margot Fonteyn, performing Tchaikovsky's *Swan Lake*. The dancers, no more than three or four inches tall, moved with breathtaking grace, their miniature Bolshoi transporting me to another world.

Mesmerized, I watched them every night for a month—from their opening performance to their poignant farewell. On the last evening, before the final curtain fell, the dancers climbed onto my bed, their delicate forms illuminated by the moonlight streaming through the window.

"Next year, we'll return," they said in voices as soft as the rustling of leaves. "Perhaps you'll join us. We'll make you younger, just four inches tall, and we'll travel through secret tunnels to ancient places, performing plays, ballets, and music."

I drifted off to sleep, my heart light with the promise of adventure, journeying to the place where dreams are born and where eternal peace awaits. In this realm, I would sail on ships laden with wine and feasts, sing with beautiful women, and never return to this world.

The nurse found me the next morning, a serene smile on my face. Clutched in my hand was a balalaika the size of my pinky finger. My gaze was fixed on the closet door, open just a crack, as though I had been watching something extraordinary until the very end.

Life Spared

AFTER WORLD WAR II ENDED IN 1945, ALL THE SURVIVING SOLDIERS returned to the United States. Among them was Mathias Damian, who made his way back to Texas. After spending a few years in Odessa, the scars of the war still fresh in his mind, he decided to seek a new beginning. He moved south to the small town of Santa Bárbara, Chihuahua, in Mexico, where distant relatives offered him a place to stay.

The town was quiet, nestled between the mountains, and life seemed slower, simpler. He moved in with an elderly couple, who took him in without question. Their daughter, María, was lovely in an unassuming way, and soon enough, Mathias married her. But despite the peaceful surroundings, the horrors of the war lingered in his mind, haunting his every waking hour. The memories of battlefields, of lives lost, gnawed at him, festering like an open wound.

One tragic night, around three in the morning, the shadows inside his home grew too much for him to bear. The madness inside him, the broken pieces of his soul, came rushing to the surface. In a brutal frenzy, Mathias murdered his wife, his in-laws—anyone in reach. The neighbors, awakened by the screams, called the police, but by the time they arrived, the damage had already been done.

Mathias was found drenched in blood, his face contorted with rage and fear, like a cornered beast. His eyes, wild and frantic, seemed to plead for an escape that he knew would never come. The newspapers, never shy of reporting violence, avoided the grisly details of that night. They simply referred to him as the "human vampire," a monster whose actions defied explanation.

The police arrived just as the mob began to form outside. Fearing the wrath of an angry crowd, they quickly subdued him. A doctor arrived, and the following morning, Mathias was injected with a lethal substance to ensure he wouldn't escape justice, and to quell any further violence.

Amid the chaos, one small life had been spared—a baby boy, found untouched in his crib, still peacefully asleep. Antonio Rodriguez was his name. He grew up with little memory of that night but carried with him a haunting mystery—the legacy of the brutal killings that had claimed his family.

Antonio would go on to become Sharp Shooter, a detective known for his sharp instincts and unwavering determination. He would eventually take on the world's most notorious criminals.

Sharp Shooter

SHARP SHOOTER WAS GRAPPLING WITH DEEP DEPRESSION AFTER losing his only son in a tragic accident in South America. He partly blamed himself for the loss, haunted by guilt over the time he hadn't spent with his son. As a hunter of killers, his work often kept him away from his family for long stretches, a sacrifice he now deeply regretted. One afternoon, he drank himself into unconsciousness. The hotel manager found him and rushed him to the hospital, his pulse faint. On the way there, Sharp Shooter awoke in a desolate city, where he crossed paths with a Pakistani killer. The man bragged about killing over a hundred children and claimed he had been sent to this place while his fate was being decided.

Sharp Shooter asked where they were. The man replied that it wasn't purgatory, hell, or heaven. No, it was a dreadful place where they were killed every day, only to be resurrected the next. The best course of action was to find a secure place to escape the hordes of one-meter-tall demons, who would torture them endlessly. Before vanishing, the Pakistani told Sharp Shooter to find a safe building.

"Seal off all the entrances, and you might survive for a while."

Sharp Shooter asked why he was there, but the man didn't answer. Instead, he said, 'I am a hawk in the service of His Majesty.' When Sharp Shooter looked again, the strange figure had vanished, leaving him alone in a city where sunlight was a thing of the past.

In the distance, he saw a cloud moving along the ground— a swarm of about twenty thousand demons, dragging two hundred people who were bound. Suddenly, they began to devour them. Some managed to escape, hiding wherever they could. One of them ran to Sharp Shooter, pleading for shelter.

"I didn't mean to kill myself; I just took too many lines, and now I'm stuck in this hell."

Sharp Shooter stood firm in front of Satan's army. "Stop, you damned demons! Don't abuse your power, you hellish creatures!" Everyone was bewildered; they couldn't understand why this man wasn't afraid. He drew two automatic pistols from their holsters and gunned down about twenty cursed dwarves. Nearly thirty doomed souls gathered behind him. The demonic beings stepped aside. In addition to his bravery, Sharp Shooter possessed something divine— something even he didn't understand.

He led the condemned to an abandoned hundred-story building. "We're going to fortify ourselves here. Block all the entrances with barricades and furniture, and keep your faith strong, because they'll be back tomorrow."

Everyone looked at him with respect, fear, and shame. He shouted at them, "It's fine! It's fine to be afraid and respectful, I accept that, but why are you ashamed?"

They all lowered their heads; only one spoke. "We're suicides. We've all offended the Almighty, except you; we still don't know why you're here."

Some said Sharp Shooter hadn't directly killed himself, that it was a mistake, and that he should be forgiven. Others said that blaspheming against the Creator and taking one's life didn't deserve forgiveness. Only the Archangel Michael advocated for him: "This servant of humanity deserves absolution; it wasn't suicide, it was a mistake. I will take my plea to the highest divine being, the one who can forgive any sin, and if I obtain forgiveness, I will descend into the hidden hells with my shining sword to rescue him."

Meanwhile, Sharp Shooter watched from the top of the building. Several clouds of soulless beings were approaching, aiming to break in not through the first floor, but through the third and fourth. That's when the terror began. He ordered all the entrances to be sealed from the tenth floor down, but he soon realized his army of suicides was full of cowards, who preferred to help the demons in hopes of being forgiven.

"Cowards! Failures! Don't be afraid! You're here because fear defeated you, cornered you. Now is the time to seek forgiveness and eternal peace." But it was too late. Nearly a thousand sadistic dwarves had infiltrated the building. Sharp Shooter exhausted his bullets on more than seventy demons, leaving him with only his Cossack saber, which, according to legend, contained metal from the lance that a Roman centurion had used to pierce the Nazarene's side. As soon as he wielded his sword, the satanic creatures fled, howling.

The worst part was that all the suicides had abandoned him, joining the cursed hordes— except for two young men who fought with bayonets affixed to old World War I rifles. Sharp Shooter stood in a warehouse, his back to the wall.

"*Vade Retro Satana!*" he shouted in Latin to ward off the demon. Exhausted, covered in the putrid blood of the demons, he was being slowly surrounded by the infernal plague. He then said to the young men, "Kneel! Beg the Almighty for forgiveness, as it's our last hope."

"We beg for forgiveness, You who gave sight to the blind and fed the multitudes, grant us mercy."

At that moment, from the center of the building, and descending from the sky, a luminous ray struck the floor. From there emerged—or descended—a beautiful man with a sword of blinding silver light. Dressed as an ancient Roman soldier, his curly blond hair flowed as one with his sword as it tore through demons, who fled while shouting obscenities.

The angel, as Sharp Shooter supposed, was the Archangel Michael, the only one who destroyed demons. Saint Michael spoke in Latin, Greek, and Old Spanish. He instructed them to stay behind him for protection and said, "Your faith has saved you, and you have been given another chance."

At that moment, Sharp Shooter awoke in a hospital, having just had his stomach pumped.

"Doctor, why did it take so long to revive me?" The doctor replied, "No, Mr. Sharp Shooter, it was only a few hours, and you were never dead. Michael Martínez, the hotel manager, stayed with you the whole time."

"Where is he, so I can thank him?"

The hotel manager was never seen again, nor were the two young men from his nightmare. Many years later, in a documentary, Sharp Shooter saw two young men assisting Mother Teresa of Calcutta. They were the same men who had been forgiven for their faith. They worked in a leper colony, doing so only for food and to show their gratitude to the Creator.

Sharp Shooter in Venezuela

GUSTAVO WORKED AT THE GENERAL HOSPITAL IN CARACAS. OF GERMAN descent, he had been born under an unusual prediction: a fortune teller told his mother that, out of all the babies delivered that month at the pediatric hospital, he would be the only one to survive. Shortly after, seventeen infants contracted a bacterial infection and perished—Gustavo was the only one to survive. They managed to cure him, but the illness left its mark, disfiguring one side of his face.

At night, Gustavo also worked in the morgue of the same hospital. It was far from pleasant, as everyone there was a sociopath. The bodies were often beaten or mutilated by the staff. But whenever the cop known as Sharp Shooter, the killer of killers, showed up, everything fell silent. Whether this was for better or worse, no one could say.

"Boys," the officer with dark skin and curly brown hair would say, "when I bring you a client, you treat him with respect. I don't want him more messed up than how I left him."

Sharp Shooter had a habit of placing a bullet right between the eyes, never leaving a mark on the back of the skull. Since his mother's murder, his sole focus had been to become the chief of his police precinct and eliminate as many criminals as possible—twenty-seven so far. Gustavo told me this story while we were drinking moonshine.

"In Caracas, the crime rate plummeted. Sharp Shooter was the lone avenger. He put an end to the violence. People feared and respected him."

Gustavo also mentioned that one day, Sharp Shooter went to Mexico to track down some Colombian human traffickers who also trafficked in child organs, and he got lost in a rural village. Rumor had it that someone slipped him a drug during a cockfight. He stayed there for days, clutching a rooster in his hand until he finally came to his senses—without money, without his gun, and completely disoriented.

Gradually, he fully regained his senses and wandered into the jungles of Chiapas, never truly remembering who he had been. He became a farmer, and no one ever heard from him again.

Sharp Shooter in Ciudad Juárez

ATIP FROM AN INFORMANT LED HIM TO CRUCIAL INFORMATION. SHARP Shooter made his way to downtown Ciudad Juárez, Chihuahua, Mexico, visiting the cathedral before stopping by "The Iron Soldier," the shop where he stocked up on ammunition and had his guns cleaned. He had a .38 called "The Black Beast," a .45 like the ones used by Mexican army soldiers, and a "Lucky Shot," a silver-plated, two-shot Derringer .22. He also carried a dragon-handled dagger that had saved him more times than he could count.

In the early hours of the morning, he set out on the road to Casas Grandes. As he drove, his eyes scanned the terrain, always alert. He spotted a rundown shack in the distance, a front for illegal activities, and entered through several tunnels.

Inside, he encountered a Japanese princess, an exquisite beauty, dressed in a kimono. She was surrounded by yakuza, their hands resting on their katanas, while Sharp Shooter's fingers hovered near his guns. The princess, sensing the tension, smiled and calmed her bodyguards. She didn't understand why he was there, warning him to avoid certain rooms. But Sharp Shooter didn't listen.

He opened the first door and found a room filled with torture devices from the Inquisition: the Rack, the Judas Chair, and the skull crusher. Realizing his mistake, he quickly exited. Behind the second door were several chained angels. He freed them, allowing some to fly away, while others, whose wings had been clipped, stayed and became men of God as their wings regrew.

In the next room, the yakuza blocked his way. With their katanas drawn, they gestured for him to open the next door. Sharp Shooter complied, and five menacing figures burst out. He fired instantly, taking down three of them. The blood from their skulls stained the filthy floors of the old house, which was riddled with tunnels dating back to the Cristero War. Sharp Shooter rescued the woman the thugs had been trying to abduct.

"What's your name?" Sharp Shooter asked.

"Sarah Marie… We need to get out of here!"

Before leaving, Sharp Shooter collected a handful of quill pens, later gifting them to composers and writers who would go on to achieve fame with their songs and books.

He drove Sarah Marie to a recovery center in Las Cruces, New Mexico, before the police could arrive and twist the story. "They'll help you here," he said. "I've got to go back; two of them got away."

"Thank you, officer. May God watch over you," Sarah Marie replied.

Sharp Shooter vanished into the night, driving his custom-modified car. The scent of death still lingered in his mind, and he muttered to himself, "I've still got two men to hunt down. I'll find them, even if it takes forever."

He disappeared into the Samalayuca Sand Dunes, the sun rising as he continued his pursuit. He didn't find them, but he never lost their trail. Meanwhile, the killings in Ciudad Juárez began to decline.

Sharp Shooter's relentless pursuit of justice continued, but as for Sarah Marie, her life took a quieter turn. With the immediate danger behind her, she sought peace and a new beginning in Las Cruces, blending into the ordinary rhythm of life. Not much was heard about Sharp Shooter after that.

Sharp Shooter and the Butcher of Rostov

IN RUSSIA, A COUNTRY KNOWN FOR ITS COMMUNIST PAST, A SURGE OF crimes, assaults, and murders involving women, teenagers, and children erupted. Despite the passage of time, there was no trace of the rapist-murderer. All efforts had been exhausted, yet the list of young victims continued to grow, and the killer remained elusive. The Russian authorities were forced to swallow their pride and seek help from the Americans, who had recently developed a new system for locating criminals.

The Federal Bureau of Investigation (FBI) had created a novel DNA identification method, designed not only to identify criminals but also to determine their motives, locations, and other crucial details. Serial killers were classified into four categories: hedonistic, visionary, mission-oriented, and authoritative.

This method, called "Profiles," was an innovation developed by the Americans. However, due to the nature of the crimes in Russia, they had to enlist Sharp Shooter, the renowned universal detective specializing in "wild beasts," serial killers, and psychopaths.

Sharp Shooter explained: "These individuals are as physically strong as a thirty-year-old man but as cunning as someone fifty years their senior. They are as sly and elusive as foxes, skilled in their actions and words, always playing mind games. They cannot distinguish between right and wrong; they act with cold, calculated precision rather than emotion. They possess exceptional intelligence, reflexes, and discipline, all within their self-created parameters."

Given his extensive experience, Sharp Shooter agreed to collaborate with the FBI on the condition that his name would not be mentioned in the media or on social networks.

In Russia, Sharp Shooter and a team of Russian and American agents focused their search in an area with a radius of ten to twenty miles. This was where the victims had disappeared, and their desecrated bodies had been discovered—close to fifty women, teenagers, and children. Sharp Shooter deduced that the killer was likely a respectable-looking individual, an authoritative figure capable of commanding the obedience of the teenagers.

During an investigation at a train station, Sharp Shooter encountered a seemingly pleasant teacher, dressed in a tie and thick glasses. The detective immediately informed the Russian authorities that this man was the rapist-murderer they were seeking. For several days, the suspect was interrogated, key questions were asked, and DNA analysis was conducted using the "Profiles" method. It was eventually confirmed that this was indeed the man they were looking for. When inquired about his family, he claimed they were not involved in the crimes.

Andréi Chikatilo, the Butcher of Rostov—as the media had dubbed him—was accused of over fifty-six murders but was found guilty of fifty-three. He was sentenced to death and executed with a single gunshot to the head.

When international media reported on the capture of the Butcher of Rostov, the credit was attributed solely to the FBI. Sharp Shooter's name was never mentioned.

Note: This story is partly based on real events, but certain details and aspects have been fictionalized by the author for narrative purposes.

Sharp Shooter and the Butcher of Odessa

THE MURDERS OF WOMEN IN CIUDAD JUÁREZ, CHIHUAHUA, MEXICO, had nearly ceased. Now, the owners of the factories were sending their most attractive female workers to factories in Texas, United States, where they would never be heard from again. Besides being attractive, they had to be orphans, so no one would miss them. These young women came from rural areas, with little education. The only requirements were youth and beauty.

While investigating, the relentless detective Sharp Shooter observed women's corpses, mutilated with katanas—traditional Japanese swords. It was well known that some factory owners were from Japan.

The killer, who dismembered his victims, was the son of a Texan billionaire who owned oil wells. A "trust fund kid" known for spending—rather, squandering—his father's fortune, he had a difficult-to-understand fetish. It was clear from miles away that he was not entirely in his right mind. (By their deeds, you shall know them…). In conversations with his associates, he would mention something about "bushes": "In the early hours, after three, shadows detach themselves to walk through the cursed streets full of malice and decay—shadows that bring terror and pain. The grinding of teeth comes to shine, ha, ha, ha!"

Sharp Shooter had heard rumors about this killer—dubbed the Butcher of Odessa. He had been trying to locate him for a while without success; the criminal was always one step ahead, as if he could enter another dimension, or like the mythical Bigfoot, always managing to evade everyone.

When he finally tracked him down, it was at a funeral home. Sharp Shooter wanted to go in alone, without local police backup. What he found left him astounded: at the back of the place, there were a hundred children being sold on the dark web! Their destination was countries like Israel, where dangerous and harmful substances in the water could damage kidneys. The traffickers used Mexican children for organ trafficking. It is well known that hundreds of children and teenagers disappear in Mexico every year. Also, on that clandestine property, there were a dozen young women held captive for exploitation and lust. When he got bored, the Butcher of Odessa would resort to torture and brutality to kill them.

The psychopath wore an amulet that supposedly transported him to ancient England in 1888, to the time of Jack the Ripper, or to the future, in the year 2666. In an improbable twist, the butcher was at that moment in Odessa, Texas—about four hundred fifty miles from Ciudad Juárez—carrying out his mad schemes.

When Sharp Shooter confronted him, a showdown between them became inevitable. It was an unarmed confrontation, a test of skill and physical strength. Sharp Shooter had him on the ground after the first few blows, tied him up, and managed to rescue the women and children from the dungeons. Next, he destroyed the amulet that the butcher claimed transported him through time, to prevent the criminal from escaping. After that, he left the butcher without hands or feet, shouting:

"So you can feel what your female victims felt!"

The psychopath writhed on the floor in pain.

Sharp Shooter asked the women to call the police:

"Don't mention me, your avenging angel! Take care of the children if you can, get them home, and may God protect you."

The detective vanished again, and within hours, he was back at El Chamizal Federal Public Park in Ciudad Juárez.

The Dark City

THE CHILDREN KEPT DISAPPEARING—FIRST TEN, THEN A HUNDRED— and no one knew where they were going. The tragic events in Ciudad Juárez, Mexico, had long since faded from public discourse.

People said the world was shrinking due to climate change, but the truth was that a world without children was a world without a future. Parents no longer searched for them or missed them, simply saying, 'Whatever God wills.

Rumors spoke of cities deep beneath the earth, where children were supposedly sent to build mythological realms. Only one detective, known as Sharp Shooter, had dared to investigate what was really happening. In Venezuela, South America, he had killed seventeen criminals with a single shot to the forehead. In Colombia, he dispatched forty-nine rapists with the same deadly precision. His mere presence in the southern regions caused assaults to decline. In Mexico, he became famous for his cunning in capturing The Jalapa Rapist.

The story, in broad strokes, unfolded in Jalapa, Veracruz. A young girl had been assaulted in a blue car by a masked man missing the ring finger on his left hand. Sharp Shooter set up roadblocks throughout the area, estimating he was only two hours behind the perpetrator. They found the car abandoned near a train station, along with the mask. Sharp Shooter waited on the other side. A professor got off the train, sweating nervously, wearing a hat and carrying a briefcase, blending in with the crowd of about a hundred people disembarking. Sharp Shooter spotted him.

"Stop him!"

"What's going on? This is outrageous!" protested the man.

"Take off your gloves!"

And sure enough, he was missing a finger on his left hand. Sharp Shooter ordered him to be drowned in a nearby stream.

"Mercy, it's a mistake! And besides, the girl provoked me!"

Sharp Shooter's motto was: "Murderers and rapists must be executed instantly, without mercy, and if there's a mistake, may God forgive us."

Antonio Rodríguez, also known as Sharp Shooter, traveled to Ciudad Juárez in search of a lost civilization. He prepared to embark on a journey to the center of the earth. But as he entered the post office, a wave of dizziness washed over him, and he struggled to leave.

The world he had known just moments ago had vanished, leaving him in a realm of shadows. He realized he had crossed into another dimension—he had found the gateway to another world.

He arrived at a truck stop, having wandered for days without seeing light or people. His hunger and thirst barely registered. He came upon a small diner, once bustling with customers, but now empty, their meals left untouched on the tables. He couldn't understand why no one was there to speak to. That night, he slept in the subway. Trains passed by him all night long, but they were empty. It was there he realized where the lost children had gone—and why. Their innocent souls. 'Is that why I'm here? What is a murderer like me doing in a place meant for good and noble souls? Where am I?' And then, suddenly, his brother Xavier appeared beside him."

"Brother, what are you doing here?"

"I came to help you in this moment of crisis."

"Where am I?"

"In a wonderful place. Enjoy it."

"Where are the children?"

"I don't know."

At that moment, his brother vanished, and he never saw him again.

He ventured into a high school, where he spoke with an old man.

"Where am I?"

"You're in another world, with different rules."

"But am I alive?"

"Just barely. In the three days you've been here, four years have passed in your world. You had a stroke."

"Will I survive? Will I return?"

"No one knows. Only the Almighty. If you want to live, it depends on Him and you. Pray to Him."

"God, my Father, I want to return to my world, to my mind and my body."

That afternoon, he was transferred from intensive care to a recovery room.

"You're out of danger. In a few days, you'll be going home. Your brain has been resting and hasn't suffered any damage."

In his mind, Sharp Shooter pondered: "Sometimes I dream of a dark city, devoid of sunlight or dawns, only shadows. I walk through parking lots, each filled with thousands of old cars. Sometimes, a child with an angelic face follows me. He stays close, seeking my protection. In my dream, I lie down to sleep on a doorstep and wake up with the little angel in my arms. I want to leave him behind, but I realize that in this city, we've both been abandoned. The cold seeps into our bones. The child wakes up, smiles at me, and offers me a crust of bread. Over time, I come to understand that this child is me, that I must take care of him. The dark city and the child are all parts of me."

The Zone of Silence

SHARP SHOOTER WAS ON THE HUNT FOR INDIVIDUALS WHO HAD FLED to Casas Grandes, Chihuahua, suspected of being involved in a conspiracy to abduct and murder children and women—people they deemed unworthy of life.

His search led him deep into the Triangle, a mysterious region spanning parts of Jiménez in Chihuahua, and the states of Coahuila and Durango. In this area, watches, compasses, and cell phones malfunction, and strange occurrences are frequent. Locals call it the Zone of Silence.

Stories about this place abound, but one fact stands clear: inexplicable phenomena happen here. Among the locals, there are whispers of tall, pale men with diamond-like eyes who have been seen wandering the area.

Sharp Shooter continued his investigation, following the faintest traces of these individuals. His pursuit eventually brought him to a community near a lake, where he encountered the strange beings who spoke in broken, unfamiliar Spanish. They gathered around him.

"We've heard of you, Sharp Shooter, the hunter of killers. But you won't find them here. My brothers and I protect this community. We have houses for vampires who feed on blood; they are locked up at night. The hairy ones—werewolves—are also confined. Pedophiles are tortured and eliminated. We don't allow women-killers to live, so they never make it here. Bigfoot creatures sometimes slip out of our dimension, but we always bring them back. They're not dangerous, but their appearance frightens people. They're humans who didn't fully evolve, stuck between animal and man. If you're looking for pedophiles, one is in the clergy, and another is in politics."

Following their cryptic advice, Sharp Shooter uncovered a cardinal with his harem of children and girls—horribly mutilated, missing limbs and tongues. Sharp Shooter wasted no time, delivering a precise shot that struck the back of the cardinal's neck. The other pedophile, having stolen from the nation, had fled to Europe, escaping justice for the time being.

The Catastrophe

T**HE YEAR WAS 2113. OVER A CENTURY HAD PASSED SINCE ANTONIO** Rodríguez, known as Sharp Shooter, the terror of criminals, had mysteriously vanished. Now, a descendant of this legendary killer hunter was living in Europe, searching deep in the Roman catacombs for a criminal.

Suddenly, a shadow of black smoke spread across the globe, blinding ninety percent of the population. Only the remaining ten percent—those living on islands, in remote mines, or otherwise hidden—were spared from the toxic environmental smoke.

The cause of the catastrophe was believed to be the eruption of the Yellowstone supervolcano, which buried nearly all of the United States in ash and smoke from the Tertiary Era. The volcanic eruption sent a thick cloud of ash across the planet, wreaking havoc on the environment. Many theories about the event remained unexplained.

The descendant of Sharp Shooter, now burdened with the task of survival, embarked on a cruise. The ship's captain was blind, and the admiral had only one eye. After a long and grueling journey, they arrived at a place where millions were in desperate need. It became easier to track down those who thrived on blood and torture, the remnants of a brutal world.

The few surviving villains were the ones who had once spread terror among the vast population. Creatures from the Mesozoic and Tertiary eras began to resurface—prehistoric men from Neanderthal and Cro-Magnon, thought to be long extinct, but now more subdued. The world had been shattered by the effects of the cataclysm, and many perished from natural causes.

An army, led by Sharp Shooter's descendant, fought to eradicate the "bad blood." Angels and cherubim descended from the heavens, bringing peace to the land. Humanity was reduced to fewer than a million inhabitants, and the world began to settle into greater tranquility.

It was then that someone remembered their mother's words: "Every cloud has a silver lining."

Good years arrived, bringing peace and joy to the few who remained, and they learned to cherish the quiet, rebuilding a world that had once been lost.

About the Author

BORN UNDER THE PARRAL SKY IN CHIHUAHUA, MEXICO, JORGE A. Ontiveros embarked on a transformative journey at the age of seventeen that led him to the vibrant culture of East Los Angeles, California. There, he navigated the hallways of Roosevelt High School, setting the stage for an academic path that took him to East Los Angeles College and California State University, Northridge. With a bachelor's degree in Hispanic Literature and a specialization in Humanities, Ontiveros's intellectual pursuits reflect both his depth of knowledge and commitment to his craft. Now residing in Oxnard, California, a coastal city where the rhythm of the ocean and the quietude of rural landscapes inspire his writing, Ontiveros crafts stories that weave together the everyday and the mysterious. As a writer, he has ventured into the labyrinthine world of fiction, becoming the author of three books in Spanish, one bilingual poetry collection, and a Micro-Fiction Anthology in English. His mystery short story collections invite readers on journeys through intricate, suspense-filled worlds, each one a reflection of his boundless imagination.

www.ingramcontent.com/pod-product-compliance
Lightning Source LLC
Chambersburg PA
CBHW040229170726
48295CB00014B/852